A Wolf's Deception

Black Hills Wolves 55

By
TL Reeve

Copyright © 2016 by TL Reeve
ISBN: 978-1-68361-110-3
Cover art by Fiona Jayde

Published by
Decadent Publishing Company, LLC

Look for us online at:
www.decadentpublishing.com

~A Note from the Author~

Dear Reader,

Thank you for purchasing a copy of A Wolf's Deception, Graham and Elle's story. When I wrote their story, I wasn't sure about the twists and turns it would take. Their story started ten years ago. And, now, they are different wolves, trying to find their proper place in life. I hope you enjoy their story. FYI, Lily and Chris are next up, along with a few new characters and some you already know and love.

As always, if you'd like to leave a review, it's appreciated. If you have any questions, please email me: **authortlreeve@hotmail.com**

TL

Dedication

To you, the reader, thank you.

Chapter One

"**L**adies, it's time." Fern tapped her finger against the scarred wooden table situated near the bar in The Den. Today, they would pick a new set of victims...er, matches. She grinned to herself, quite chuffed at their impressive record. All those matches made. All those mates finally getting past the bullshit. *About damn time, if you ask me.*

"Who's on the docket for today?" Lonnie waved Paul over to them.

Such a good boy. Her heart clenched. After the last alpha cut the boy's tongue out, she'd worried about him. On more than one occasion, she'd wondered if he'd ever find his place within the pack. He spent so much of his life in silence and alone. Then, he met his mate, PG. It was like watching the boy be born again. He chatted in sign language nonstop now, and who was she to stop him?

"I thought we would work on Jason," Fern said. Since Claire's son had come home, he'd been a little reluctant to get out and socialize. Cute as a button, he needed a firm hand, and she had the man for him.

"That boy." Claire tsked. "So shy. I have no idea where he gets it. Certainly not me or his father."

"Obviously," Kathy piped up. "Didn't we see you running through the woods last night?"

Her friend blushed. "Joe had a wild hair."

"Your mate had a wild something," Lonnie said. "Could hear him howling from our back porch."

They laughed.

"Well...." Claire shrugged. "When you've got it. You've got it."

Another round of laughter ensued.

When Paul stopped beside them, Fern ordered. "A beer and burger for each of us. We need brain fuel."

He gave a curt nod. *Coming up.*

After he stepped away from them, Fern leaned in. "I have the man for Jason. I think he'll piss kittens when he meets the guy, but they'll be good for each other."

"Oh?" Her best friend's brow rose. "Do tell."

"Hombre." She'd only caught a glimpse of him a couple of times, working on a bike at the rundown shop near the edge of Hill City. Hombre had come to them after Gabby got herself in a good pickle. That boy would do anything to protect her, especially after she was kidnapped along with Fawn and Tinks. The man had a loyal streak a mile wide, and she had a feeling he'd fit right in. Though Gabby's extended family lived off pack lands, they were gossiped about on a daily basis. Who wouldn't talk about them? All were huge, burly men, covered in tattoos, and had surly dispositions to boot. Then there was Alicia. The beautician had worked wonders on Fern's hair a time or two, of which Henry approved.

"The big biker from Hill City?" Kathy sat forward, her hands clasped together.

"Yes. Why not?"

"He might chew Jason up and spit him out." Skepticism filled her words as she sat back in her chair.

"Well, that wouldn't be so bad, would it?" She arched a brow. "He's protective to a fault. Loyal. He's got the qualities we'd look for in any of our matches."

When Paul returned with their meals, she paused the conversation so they could eat. She had no doubt Jason and Hombre would make a great pair. They just needed a chance...the right circumstances to bring them together.

The bar door opened, a shaft of light glaring inside. Fern dragged her attention from her food to find Graham Truesdale striding toward them. She frowned.

The last she'd heard, his little mate had passed away. "Poor thing." She pitched her voice low to keep from drawing his attention. "Having his mate die so young."

Kathy nodded. "Such a tragedy."

He fist-bumped Paul when the man handed over a large paper bag. Graham had been on lunch duty for a couple of weeks now, getting Gabby and Fawn something to eat since both women were getting further along in their pregnancies. Seemed like every day, that boy was going from Los Lobos Café to Dottie's, the diner, or The Den, grabbing something for either woman. She remembered being pregnant. Her cravings had been off the chart. The rawer and spicier, the better. She must have driven Henry crazy with the concoctions she hankered for.

Bag in hand, he walked toward the door. *He'll have to go on the list, too.*

Claire shook her head and tsked. "I still can't believe how much devesta—"

"She's not dead." Gee's deep voice resounded from behind the bar.

"What?" Setting her burger down, she angled toward him. Everyone knew what happened. Had seen the aftermath of it. "What are you saying?"

The bear shifter continued wiping down the bar top. "I said, she's not dead."

Lonnie pushed away from the table. "Where is she? If I find out you've known all along, I'll—"

"Ask your nephew." He gestured at Kathy with his rag. "He knows all about it."

Kathy narrowed her eyes. "Oh, he does, does he?"

Fern struggled not to grin. With her friend on the warpath, the pack enforcer didn't stand a chance. *And Ryker has no clue his aunt's coming for him. This is going to be good.*

After dabbing the corners of her mouth, Kathy tossed her napkin next to her plate, her barely contained fury palpable. Fern set her napkin down, too. *Batten down the hatches. We're at DEFCON three.*

"Ladies," Kathy said in a clipped tone, "I believe a field trip is in order. Gee, keep our lunch warm."

He grunted. "He's at the house with Saja. I don't think he'll want to be interrupted."

"What you think and what he's going to explain are two different things." She smacked her palm against the table and rose from her seat. "How dare he keep this important piece of information from us."

Fern and the other two pack matrons followed suit. *DEFCON two, ladies.*

The bear sighed.

Kathy, along with the other matrons, stormed Ryker's house. Saja's giggles and the thick scent of their mating hung in the air. She was happy for them. A new pup with enforcer genes, and more than likely a dominant streak a mile wide, warmed her heart. *But when will the boy learn he has a duty to this pack? If he's going to help someone get away from a brutal alpha, bringing them home is paramount.* Angry at the situation, she was of a mind to snatch him by his ear and bring him all the way to the Truesdale homestead to explain what happened. However, she refrained. No need in causing Saja any undue stress. Banging on the door, she stepped back.

"Go the fuck away," Ryker growled.

She pounded on the door again. "Ryker Grey, get your ass out here, and don't you dare cuss at me."

He cursed again, and the soft thuds of a scrambling wolf brought a smile to her face. When the door opened, his large frame filled the entryway, his hair tousled, his cheeks flushed. She'd laugh if the situation hadn't been so serious. "What can I do for you?"

"Elle St. Claire."

His features remained blank.

"Don't you dare block me out." She waggled her finger at him. "Where is she?"

He crossed his arms. "Safe."

She snorted. "Don't pull that with me."

"She is. What is so important you need to know her whereabouts?"

"Boy, you're lucky I can't reach your ear, or else I'd snatch you out of there."

"Hi, Kathy." Saja stuck her head out of the doorway. "Everything okay?" Her hand went to her belly, rubbing it along the side.

"Fine, dear." Though she softened her reply, she kept her gaze locked with Ryker.

He cracked a smile. "No, you won't."

She lifted her chin. "I am not leaving you alone until you bring Elle home." *The girls have my back. They'll stay with me, however long it takes my hardheaded nephew to come to his senses.*

He stared at her a moment more. After reaching into his pocket to pull out his phone, he pushed a few buttons then held it to his ear.

"Shawn. We need to talk."

Chapter Two

Three weeks later....

G raham Truesdale drove the main road into town. *Why does Shawn Blu need my help? He's a private eye, for god's sake. What could I possibly do that he couldn't?*

For the last few weeks, he'd damn near run himself ragged. If he wasn't tending the cattle with his brother Kalum, he was getting his mated sisters Fawn and Gabby food. Their bellies seemed to grow every day, and a thread of longing filled him. He wanted what his brother and Kru had. Though he'd never say it, he envied them. Seeing them together happened to be why he spent more time in Rapid City when he wasn't working. Because he couldn't take it anymore.

He'd had a mate once, a long time ago. A little female a few years younger than he and filled with wide-eyed wonder. Had things been different, he'd have marked her. Unfortunately, she'd passed away. He still remembered the night her house burned down. He'd tried to go to Elle's house several times, and it had taken Kalum and their father to hold him back. The wolf rose up inside of him, demanding he go to her, yet they wouldn't allow it.

If you go, son, your death is assured. His father's words had knocked a bit of sense into him, but it hadn't stopped the endless pacing. Or the gut-wrenching pain he experienced day after day. Her tragic death had been the catalyst for his parents leaving pack lands. They wouldn't sit by and allow a madman to torment them any longer. He was thankful every day that his mom and dad took him out of the pack and far away from their home. He attributed his ability to stay sane to their move. He should have told them Elle died, he supposed, but it wouldn't have served any purpose—then or now. So, he tried to move on and hoped beyond everything he'd get a second chance at finding a mate.

He pulled up to the row of repaired shop fronts, parking his truck along the curb. Shawn Blu's business sat between Los Lobos Café and Los Lobos Books and More. In the last year, tons of work had been done to rebuild the rundown town, though not much had been done to the local PI's office.

He got out of his truck, and grimaced. The sun glinted off the dirty windows, doing nothing to make the place appear less fly-by-night. The only thing going for it, at the moment, was the painted placard hanging over the door. *If Shawn's serious about his new business, he needs to spruce the place up. Make it look appealing to those who need his help.*

After a quick tap on the door, he opened it and stepped inside.

The PI sat behind his desk, phone in hand, talking to someone about a location for a pack member. Shawn glanced up and grinned when Graham stepped farther into the space. The floors needed a good sanding and some varnish. A lone fake tree sat in the corner across from his desk, and the walls were a musty yellow color from years of neglect. *Yep, the guy really needs to invest in the place before he runs off potential clients.*

Holding his finger up to Graham, Shawn finished his call. "When you have the info, let me know...thanks." He pushed the end button then motioned for him to sit in the only available chair. "Take a seat. I'm glad you could make it."

"Not a problem. I'm a little surprised you asked for my help." He sat down in the chair across from him. "What can I do for you?"

"There is a bus arriving in Hill City today at noon. A pack member is coming home. I'd do it myself, but I have a few other leads I need to follow up on." He scribbled something on a note pad, ripped the sheet off, and handed it to him.

"Bus number?"

Shawn nodded. "Yes and where she departed from. Charlotte, North Carolina."

"Great." He folded the slip of paper in half then placed it in his pocket. "Anything else I should know about?"

"She might be a little skittish. She never thought she'd be returning after everything she's been through."

He nodded. In the beginning, after his parents left all those years ago, he'd never thought they'd return either. Amazing what ten years and the death of a power-hungry ruthless, alpha did to change your perspective on everything. They'd returned last summer and begun rebuilding their home, making it what it once was, their mom and dad's pride and joy. "Not a problem. I think we all understand her."

"You're right. She'll be staying at Miss Kathy and Clyde's place while she figures out her next move."

"All right." He glanced at his watch. "Well, I guess I should be going. Don't want to be late."

"Great." Shawn's cell rang, and he grabbed it, glancing at the screen. "I gotta take this." He looked at Graham. "Give me a call when you've picked her up, so I can let Miss Kathy know she's on the way."

"Will do."

Stepping out into the midday sun, he startled at a soft yelp. Lost in thought, he hadn't been paying attention to where he was going and bumped into Tinks. His hands came out to brace her, so she didn't fall. The eccentric artist seemingly flitted around town, helping everyone she could as she went. With her eye for art, she'd helped design some of the businesses logos, including Shawn's. Glancing down, he grinned. "Sorry 'bout that. Stupid me for not paying attention to where I was going."

"Not a problem. I swear, if my head wasn't attached to my shoulders, I'd lose it." She huffed. "Did you just come out of Shawn's office?"

He nodded.

"Didn't happen to see a fan-tipped paintbrush did you?" She searched through her bag again, pausing momentarily to push a stray lock of multicolor hair behind her ear. "I could have sworn I had it with me when I left."

"No, sorry. I didn't. But Shawn is in there for a few more minutes if you want to check with him."

"Crap. That one was expensive. Bobbi is always reminding me not to be so damn absentminded." He could only imagine the conversations she'd had with her sister. Though they'd been back for over a year, he hadn't seen the ornery woman around town. Tinks smirked, closing her bag. "I keep telling her, I'm a free spirit who can't be tamed."

He chuckled. "I believe you. I hope you find it. Hate to see you out a brush."

She gave a shrug. "I'm sure it'll turn up."

***

Elle St. Claire stared out the window of the almost-empty bus. For the past two days, and three transfers, she'd perched close to the window—the mingling scents of the other passengers drove her wolf senses insane. Some people didn't know what a bar of soap was for or how not to bathe in overpowering perfume and cologne.

As the vast rolling openness passed by, her last conversation with Shawn Blu replayed in her mind.

"But how?" She rubbed her forehead as she paced the spacious bedroom of the Charlotte mansion. She'd made sure to close the door behind her, so her fiancé, Rupert Wellington, couldn't hear her.

"Over the years, the alpha was poisoned. No one will say who, and, when Drew returned, he killed Magnum," Shawn told her. "Things have changed. It's safe now. No one will hurt you. You have nothing to fear."

Oh, she had plenty to fear. "I-I don't know. Maybe I need a few more days." She glanced down at the four-carat rock settled on her ring finger. Ten years ago, when she fled Black Hills, South Dakota, and headed east, she'd never contemplated this moment. And, heck, who'd have thought she'd be engaged to a senator's son?

"The longer you take to decide, the more ways you'll convince yourself you shouldn't do this."

Truth filled his words. "When?"

"I have a bus ticket for you. You'll leave tomorrow." The implied "don't tell anyone where you're going" hung between them. She knew the rules. However, she'd have to leave Rupert a note.

When she arrived in Charlotte, she'd had a safe home to stay in and a couple hundred dollars to her name. For the first few months, she worked under-the-table, washing dishes, babysitting for her co-workers when she needed to make ends meet. Then she met a woman who could get her a birth certificate and a social security card. With those things, she was able to better her life.

"Okay." She nibbled her bottom lip. To return home and live

with her pack again. To be among her own kind. To let her wolf run free. "I'll do it."

The bus rolled to a stop. The air brakes blew out compressed air as they locked into place, signaling she'd arrived at her destination. Standing, she waited for the others to disembark before grabbing her purse from the overhead bin. When she finally stepped off the bus, the dry heat of summer hit her. Nothing like the oppressive wetness she'd become accustomed to in Charlotte, but it still grabbed her.

She squinted, glancing around the quaint town. Ten years ago, she'd waited at the same stop for transportation out of the hills. Breathing deep, she drew in the fresh scent of wilderness and home. Her wolf pranced, overjoyed by the idea of running free once more.

Since leaving, she'd bound her wolf, only running every few months so not to draw attention to herself—a small price to pay for what little freedom she'd accrued after leaving Los Lobos. It'd been one of the reasons she'd agreed to come home, that and she had a plan. Last night, while the headlights of cars passed on the opposite side of the freeway, the soft snores of the patrons around her keeping her awake, she knew what she needed to do.

Her upcoming nuptials must be done with a clear conscience. She had to tell Rupert about her dual nature. She wanted to show him her wolf. Coming home and talking to Drew would be the first step. Once he gave her permission to bring Rupert to pack lands, she'd explain who and what she was and start their new life together with her pack. Though Rupert wanted to run for office and follow in his father's footsteps in North Carolina, he could do so in South Dakota, she assured herself.

After stepping out of the motor coach, she grabbed her overnight tote from the baggage compartment and moved away from everyone. From here, she knew the way home. Too bad she couldn't shift and run the rest of the way. Her wolf wanted to. But with her bag? Maybe not.

As she rounded the front of the bus, she stopped dead in her tracks. The scent of sandalwood and pine combined with the subtle hint of leather wafted in the air. She'd never forgotten his scent. When she was a pup, she'd have given anything to roll all over him to keep Graham's scent close to her.

Her stomach tightened as her heart lodged in her throat. *What is he doing here?* So far, he hadn't seen her.

The years had been kind to him. Tall, and rangy, he filled out those jeans to the point she wondered if he painted them on. The top three buttons of his Western-style shirt were undone, the sleeves rolled up, exposing his thickly corded forearms. His black cowboy hat sat low, shielding his eyes from the blazing sun.

Guilt lanced her gut as she stared at him. Her wolf demanded she march right over to the man and claim what was hers, yet the diamond solitaire on her ring finger stilled the hormonal response she had for the man.

You're taken. Your soon-to-be husband is all you need. Not a mate. She'd known when she met Rupert, he wasn't the one. However, she never thought she'd be returning home. Nor did she think she'd ever see Graham again. The wolf in her yearned to find the Truesdale family and go to them. But if she'd returned, Magnum would have killed her and, in turn, figured out Ryker hadn't done his job, which would have meant not only his death but put countless others at risk.

Grabbing her bag and straightening her shoulders, she headed for him. The minute he saw her, his demeanor changed. His shoulders tensed. His eyes narrowed. His whole body poised to attack—*chase.*

Her wolf hoped so. The woman...not so much.

But you're standing in front of your mate.

Not good.

How is this possible? Her scent curled around him. Sunflowers and sunshine. *She's alive. After all these years.*

His dick thickened behind the fly of his jeans. His wolf pushed forward, demanding he be let loose to claim what was rightfully his. He fisted his hands at his sides, afraid of what would happen if he touched her.

Control. He needed to grab this shit by the reins and slow down the wolf's roll. He allowed his gaze to slide over her. Still the pretty little ash-blonde beauty with curls, she hadn't changed a bit. Her big brown doe eyes drew him in. *Elle St. Claire.* He'd have questioned whether or not this was real if he hadn't been standing before her while drops of perspiration rolled down his nape. He lost all ability to speak, afraid if he did she might disappear.

"Hi." The single syllable punched him in the gut. "Long time no see."

No shit. The last time he saw her, she'd been running home after spending the afternoon with him on the farm. A few hours later, the acrid smell of burning wood and human flesh had permeated the air. Two days later, after he pleaded with his father to let him go, he saw the burned-out shell of her house. Her death, along with her mother and father's, was announced that afternoon by Ryker.

"Hi," he grunted.

She fidgeted, drawing her bottom lip between her teeth, teasing the fuck out of him. The beast within him rose again, baring his teeth, demanding he take what was rightfully his. Instead, he held himself still, forcing his wolf down. Mounting her in the middle of a crowd would cause undue attention.

"So." She fiddled with the handle of her luggage. "I guess you're here to collect me?"

"Yep."

"Do you want to go, then?" She lifted her eyebrows in question.

"Yes." He grabbed her bag and led her to his truck. After placing her bag in the bed of the vehicle, he opened the door for her. "Shouldn't take long."

"No, it shouldn't."

With a curt nod, he closed the passenger door. *Elle-fucking-St. Claire.* After all this time of him and the rest of his family being home, why hadn't someone told him the truth? Why did they keep his mate away from him? Bigger question, who the hell had known the truth about her? He slid in beside her and started the truck, dropped it into gear, and pulled away from the curb.

"Things have changed." His words came out rougher than he'd intended, but he fought a losing game with his baser instincts. Knowing he'd have to be with her for the next eleven miles, scenting her sweet aroma, might literally drive his wolf insane.

"Yeah, Shawn told me." She fidgeted, wringing her hands then twisting them in the hem of her skirt. The afternoon sunlight glinted off something on her finger as she unclenched the material.

Fuck. He pulled her hands apart—the skin-to-skin contact kicking his heart into overdrive—and glared at the sparkler adorning her ring finger. "Son of a bitch," he growled. "When did you go and get yourself married?"

Jerking free, she tucked her hands in her lap and angled away from him. "Not that it's any of your business"—Elle lifted her chin—"but I'm not married. I'm engaged to a wonderful human. His daddy's a senator."

Shit. He shifted his focus to the road. "He ain't your mate." His wolf snarled, gnashing his teeth at the thought of another man touching her. *Get your shit together.* He squeezed the steering wheel until his knuckles turned white. Taking several deep breaths, which only served to draw more of her natural perfume into his nostrils, fed his longing to have her one more day.

"We'll see." Her haughty reply challenged his assertion.

Yes, we will. "You'll be staying with Miss Kathy."

"Oh." She cleared her throat. "Okay."

They rode the rest of the way in silence, Elle staring out the passenger window, Graham not daring to ask for details he didn't want to know. Taking the turn off the highway, he followed the road into the hills.

"We'll be home shortly." As they bumped along the rutted dirt road, the conversation he'd had with his sister Lily several months ago replayed in his head.

"Why don't you ask Shawn for help to find Elle?" Lily rolled out the dough to make some of her famous biscuits.

"There's something I need to tell you." He leaned against the counter. "You were so young at the time, and Mom and Dad wanted to protect you." He took a breath. Better to just rip the Band-Aid off. "Elle's dead. Her house burned down, and her and her parents' bodies were found inside. She's never coming back."

Tears welled in his sister's eyes. She turned away, and he wanted to howl in outrage.

"I'm sorry, Lily."

The country twang of Travis Tritt's voice filled his truck. The sound jerked him out of his thoughts. Hitting the talk button, he then unhooked it from the dash clip and brought it to his ear. "Yeah?"

"Everything go okay?" Shawn asked.

"Fine. On our way. Anything else?"

"Uh," he said.

"Something wrong?"

"Why would anything be wrong? Another wolf is home. We should be celebrating." He cut his gaze to the woman occupying the seat next to him.

"O-kay, well, Miss Kathy said she's at the bookstore, and Clyde is at the house. So bring her on."

"Will do. We'll be there in about five minutes." He hit the end call button and threw his phone into the cup holder.

"You're angry."

"Nope." He drove past the gas station on the outskirts of town. "I have nothing to be mad about. Welcome home, Elle."

Chapter Three

Two days later....

G raham sat astride his paint mare as the cattle entered the chute. Half were going to slaughter to provide meat for the town, the other half to the back side of the property to graze. Two days ago, he'd dropped Elle off at Miss Kathy and Clyde's house, and, like a chicken shit bastard, he hadn't gone back to see her. He used the anger of being blindsided— along with the rock sitting on her ring finger—to explain why he stayed away.

He'd never be able to give her the same things she'd obviously become accustomed to over the years. Though his family did well for themselves, they weren't rolling in dough. They were simple ranchers, and she was a socialite. How had things changed so dramatically for them?

From the moment he saw her all those years ago, standing in a field of wildflowers, the sun casting a golden halo around her, he'd known she belonged to him. Her long, ash-blonde hair blew gently in the breeze, while her big, brown eyes glittered with arousal and mischief. Her willowy figure and pixie features did things to him. Just the thought of her made his gut clench and his heart lodge in his throat. He'd missed her something awful. Mourned her death and feared he'd die as well, of a broken heart. Yet the muscle continued to beat within his chest, a vicious reminder of the broken man he'd become.

His parents, even before Elle's house burned down, knew the potential dangers of staying while Magnum reigned supreme. Seen the damage he could inflict to the females. His mother would rather die in the human world than allow anything to happen to her baby girl or her sons. So they'd escaped. Since their parents had passed away from massive heart attacks, he and Kalum had continued to watch over their sister.

"If I didn't know any better, I'd swear something has gotten under your skin," Kalum said, not taking his eyes of the cattle. The heifers were in season, and, by the end of the week, he was sure they'd be with calf. His brother prided himself on his cattle and breeding hardy stock.

If only it was just under my skin. Nudging the mare forward, Graham stopped beside his brother then got down. "Want the truth?"

"No," Kalum drawled. "Lie to me."

He laughed, for all the wrong reasons. "What if I told you I helped Shawn bring a wolf home two days ago?"

"I'd say it was a good day for our pack. Why?"

"What if I told you it was Elle St. Claire?"

His brother's slack-jawed, wide-eyed response spoke volumes. "I don't think I heard you properly."

"You heard me just fine. Elle is alive."

"But...we saw the house. We smelled it. The bodies. We...." *Grieved.* Kalum didn't have to say it; the understanding was there.

"She got out. I'm not sure how, but she's returned." He snorted and shook his head. "And, if that's not shocking enough, she's engaged."

"What-the-ever-loving-fuck? I thought she was, *is* your mate." His brother scrubbed his face. "No wonder you look so messed up."

"Yeah, tell me about it." He set his foot on the pen's metal bar, the midmorning sun warming the back of his neck. Summer had finally come to the hills. Wildflowers dotted the area around them, adding pops of purple and pink to the yellow barberry flowers.

"You have to convince her she's making a mistake first then remind her what being your mate means." His brother's voice held absolute conviction. Since mating Fawn, Kalum had changed. He no longer existed, he lived. He reminded Graham of their father, especially when his mate looked at him.

"Maybe." Shit. He didn't know what to do. His wolf said claim her. The rational part of him said he'd lost his chance, even though he'd never really had one. The man and the beast warred for dominance inside him, leaving him even more confused and fucked up than before.

Kalum squinted as he gazed out over the pasture. "I'll give you a week."

Graham sighed. "A week?"

"Whatever you're trying to figure out, get it straight then claim your mate. Don't do something you'll regret. After all the shit that's happened in the last few months, you need to find your happiness."

Yeah. Whatever. "Sure, brother. I'll just mosey over to Miss Kathy's house, demand Elle leave her fiancé, and mate her. Why didn't I think of that?"

"Who is this guy?"

"A human. His dad's a senator or something."

"Well, shit." Kalum growled.

"She's still skittish, and I'm worried about pushing too fucking hard. Let me do this at my pace." Hell, he still hadn't had a chance to reconcile his feelings. Their reunion had started with a surprise rabbit punch to his heart followed by a running war of fury and balls-aching need. Today, he walked around bruised, battered, and in a fog of disbelief and anger.

"Well, I have no doubt you'll figure something out." Kalum's gaze cut toward the other side of the chutes where pack veterinarian and family friend, Chris Banks, gave the cows a once over then looked at Graham again. "Why don't you head back to the house and check on Fawn for me. Chris is going to be here for a couple more hours. One of the heifers is sick. Fuck knows what she got into."

He nodded. "Sure. Use the two-way radio if you need me."

After removing the tack from his horse and getting her something to eat, he made the short trek to the house. Kru's white pickup truck sat in the driveway, which meant his mate, Gabby, had arrived for her daily visit with Kalum's mate and Kru's sister, Fawn. The last few months had been a whirlwind of activity with his sister-in-law announcing her pregnancy a few weeks after Christmas and then Gabby doing the same a month later.

The cute, sassy mama had an attitude to rival most and fit Kru to a tee. The couple had endured a shit ton of stuff. Even though Graham's wounds had healed, sometimes the images of a broken, battered Gabby filtered through his mind, turning his stomach. How one human could have as much hate in his heart as Player had astounded him, though it shouldn't. The Tao pack's last alpha, Magnum, had held the same hate.

But the two women's rounding bellies was cause for hope. And with his family expanding, the urge to find a mate weighed heavy on him, or had until yesterday when he picked up Elle from the bus stop. Seeing her again awoke the beast within him, and, after dropping her off at Miss Kathy and Clyde's home, he'd headed for the trails and spent the night running.

"Don't think about it," he muttered. "It'll only fuck with your mind." He opened the door to the house then kicked off his boots.

Kip gave a happy bark from her spot near Fawn. The Border Collie had taken to her the moment they met. Fawn's feeding her scraps of bacon and other meaty delicacies might have played a role in it.

"Hey, Graham, you're early." She pushed to her feet. "Want some lunch? Lily was about to pull the fixings out for sandwiches."

"I could eat a bite." He inclined his head. "Gabby, how are you?"

"I'm a bit tired." She grinned up at him, her hand instantly going to the growing baby bump. "But the twins are doing great."

"Excellent."

"You going out tonight?" Lily stepped around him as she followed Fawn.

"Maybe." If anything, he'd shift and do some snooping, check in on Elle. If he accidentally bumped into her in town, well, what a coincidence. His wolf thought that an excellent plan.

"Aren't you tired of running around?" Lily turned on the water to wash her hands in the kitchen sink.

"What's with you and our brother?" He walked to the fridge, grabbed the pitcher of sweet tea, and placed it on the counter. "He said the same thing out in the pasture."

"Did he?" His sister arched a brow. "Well, he's right."

"Lily," he started, grabbing a glass, "I have something to tell you, but you need to...shit, it's going to be a shock."

She wiped her hands on the dish towel then laid it on the counter. "Okay, why does this sound ominous?"

Eh, because it might be? "Elle St. Claire is alive, and she's come home to Los Lobos."

***

Elle stood in front of the charred remains of her childhood home. The barren spot, devoid of any new grass or vegetation, reminded her of the night she'd been whisked away. Memories of her childhood flooded her mind—most of them intertwined with Graham and his family. *No, don't even think about it.* However, she found it hard to do. Her wolf desperately wanted out. Her wolf wanted her mate. *Sometimes what the heart wants isn't what's best for it.*

She had a duty to Rupert. She loved him. Though a busy man most days, working late and taking business trips, he cared for her, too. Gave her everything she could ever want or desire. He also gave her stability she yearned for after everything she'd been through. To leave him now would be a disservice to what they'd built. She'd invested a lot in this relationship. Besides, what did children know about mates? Or forever? Absolutely nothing. Graham had to realize the ten years they'd spent apart had changed them. They were adults now. They needed to walk away on amicable terms and not look back.

Stepping onto the wooden porch, she tested the slats in front of her for stability then moved deeper into the ruins of her former life. Images of that night filled her mind.

The wildflowers were in full bloom. Her mother would love the project she was working on. Elle bent to pick another of the flowers and contemplated which others she'd use. There were so many, and she had little space. How did one choose the prettiest flowers when they were all so beautiful? She nibbled on her bottom lip. She'd take them all. The picture would be bigger, but her mother would love it.

Hours had passed by the time she'd finally collected all the different types of flowers available to her. The walk home wouldn't take long, and when she got there, dinner would be waiting for her. She grinned.

As she came to the top of the ridge, she smelled the smoke before she saw it coming from her home. Flames licked at the windows. The place was fully engulfed. She ran straight for it, dropping the flowers at some point. Her parents were in there. She had to get to them. Deep down, she knew there was no way, but she had to try.

Unfortunately, Greer spotted her. He came straight for her, his eyes wide, crazy. He looked feral. She ran, back toward the forest. She had to hide. She had to get away from him. She wouldn't go with him. Wouldn't be his breeding machine. She headed for the densest part, knowing if she could find a hiding place, she could wait him out. Trees whipped past her. The dead leaves and needles crunched under her shoes. A stitch formed in her side; her legs grew tired. If she shifted, she'd do a hell of a lot better.

Then Ryker appeared in front of her. Energy crackled around him. "You have to run."

She stumbled backward, trying to catch her breath. "W-what?"

"Your parents are dead." His features twisted as he snarled, scaring the shit out of her. "Run. Do not stop until you reach Hill City. Use your mother's maiden name." His dark eyes narrowed, his focus snapping to the woods where her family's home lay. "Run. Now. Never return."

She ran with all her might, shifting as she jumped over a log. Her muscles protested the quick transformation. Her lungs burned as she pushed herself full tilt. When she reached Hill City, she had no clue where to go. Had she run far enough for Magnum and his men not to track her? A Greyhound Bus sign glowed in the night like a beacon.

She approached the window, tugging at the scraps of her clothes. The man at the counter looking up from some novel he'd been reading didn't appear disturbed by her state of dress, or rather undress. "I need a ticket."

"Name?"

"Elle St.— Um, Elle Adams." She nibbled her bottom lip. "But I don't have any money."

His blond eyebrows rose. Then he reached beneath the counter and drew out an envelope which he slid across the counter to her. "This is for you."

She eyed the item.

"It's all right. Take it."

She opened the envelope. Inside lay several hundred dollars. What? She lifted her gaze to his.

"Destination?"

Ryker had told her to run. Where would she be safe? "East. As far as I can go."

The grunt of a familiar bear greeted her, drew her from the dark night that had changed her life. "Why'd you come back here?"

"To remember." Her heart still ached at the loss of her parents. She missed them dearly every day, their deaths seeming so senseless. She faced Gee. "Aren't you a sight for sore eyes. Haven't even aged a bit."

He snorted. "Why do you want to remember this?" He pointed to the pile of burned lumber, aged by ten years of weather.

Elle shrugged. "My parents died here. Seemed appropriate to come back and pay my respects."

"You've spent too much time with humans. Their spirits are gone. Been gone. You lived. Move on." His gruff words held truth.

"Perhaps." Could she let go without ever knowing what happened to her parents that night? Probably not. She held up her hand. "I'm getting married."

He grunted.

"Aren't you happy for me?"

"Be happier if you'd stopped denying your wolf. Answer me this...have you thought about why you came back?"

The ruins of her home drew her focus. *Yes. To get Drew's permission to bring Rupert to Los Lobos.* They could build a house, right here, on her land. Raise a family and be happy. Childish matters of the heart had no place in her new life. This was who she had become. This was who she would be. "Yes," she answered. "I—"

When she glanced to where Gee had been standing, the place was empty. *Crazy old bear.*

Testing the floor of the house, she took a tentative step into what had been the living room. What she hoped to find or see there, she didn't know, but it felt right coming back. She eased her foot forward another step.

Rinnnng.

The sudden sound of her phone startled her. She twitched, adding pressure to the slat for balance. The charred wood gave way.

"Oh!" she yelped, falling on her rear. The incessant ringtone cut through the tirade of curses flowing her from her.

She yanked out her cell and jabbed the screen. "What?"

"Elle?" Her best friend, Kizzy Rhapsody, sounded concerned.

She closed her eyes as she pulled her foot from the hole and gingerly stood up. "Hey. What's going on?"

"Rupert is freaking out. Why didn't you tell him where you were going? He's called all of us, looking for you."

She closed her eyes. Rupert always seemed so collected and calm. To hear he'd been worried about her warmed her but also concerned her. Sure, the note she'd left had been a little vague. But she couldn't say, *Hey, I went home to be a wolf for a minute and make sure you can come with me.* "Well, you can't tell him anything."

"Pfft." Her friend laughed. "Like I would."

Breathing a sigh of relief, she stepped away from the burned-out carcass of a house. "Great. Then we shouldn't have any more issues."

"Where are you?"

"Safe. It's the only thing you need to know right now."

"Safe?" She paused. "Wait, did you run away?"

"No, Kizzy, I didn't run away. I'm fine. I just need a few days to set everything straight. I'll be home soon, promise."

"Good," her friend said. "Call me."

"I will. Don't worry."

After ending the call, she tucked her phone into her pocket and found the trail leading to town. As much as Rupert cared, he'd always been so involved with his work, his dedication leaving her on her own more often than not. Getting him to Los Lobos would slow him down, make him appreciate everything they had together.

Scrolling through the contacts on her phone, she stopped at the picture of her Rupert. Safe. Secure. His all-American good looks stared back at her.

Her finger hovered over the call button. *No. Text first.* As good as the cell coverage had been, dark spots remained. She'd hate if the call dropped in the middle of their conversation. She typed out a quick message.

Thinking of you, too. Sorry I left so fast. Don't fret. Will be home soon. ~E.

She hit send and the little squares tracked across the screen. Message sent, she continued on. Miss Kathy had mentioned a diner in town. Lunch right about now sounded perfect. After a bite, she'd see Drew.

Stick to the plan.

Caught up in her thoughts while making a list of things to ask her alpha and what kind of qualifications she could give about her fiancé, she startled when a figure stepped in front of her. She glanced up, Graham's appearance surprising her. Her wolf perked. *Mate.* Desire swamped her. "Sorry," she murmured, unable to tear her gaze from his.

"Don't be."

Okay. Well. "If you'll excuse me." She went to step around him, only to have him stop her, his hand on her forearm branding her skin.

"You're making a mistake." The snarl of contempt in his voice startled her.

"I've made plenty." She pulled free from his grasp. Her wolf howled with fury. *Mate!* She ignored it. "Tell me which one you're referring to, and I'll try to fix it later on."

"You'll never be happy without your mate."

"I've done fine for a while now," she spat. Guilt weighed on her. Her heart and wolf warred inside of her. One said duty, the other said mate.

"Damn it, Elle. You know who we are. You know we're meant to be together."

She held up her hand, showing him the ring. "I have four carats that say differently!" The minute the words left her mouth, she knew she'd made a mistake. "Let it lie. Move on. I have."

"I haven't," he growled. "A mate is for life." He crowded her, lowering his face to hers. The freckles she'd adoringly traced as a child stood out in contrast to his tanned skin. His slate-blue eyes darkened with lust. "You need to wake up from whatever fairy tale you've built for yourself. This is your life." He crushed his mouth to hers.

Fisting the front of his shirt, she meant to push him away, yet, with each swipe of his tongue along the seam of her lips, she fell deeper under the spell he wove. Unable to deny him, she opened to him. His tongue stroked against hers, coaxing her to take from him. She moaned, pressing her body to his muscular form. The thick outline of his erection fit to her hip, exciting her. His arms banded around her, and, in those few seconds, she felt safe. Secure. Wanted.

Rupert.

"No," she yelped, untangling herself from him. "We can't do this. I'm engaged!" The hysterical quality to her voice did nothing to cover the thread of desire coursing through her. "Please, stay away from me while I'm here. I'll be gone in a couple of days."

"God dammit, Elle. Stop talking about your fucking fiancé."

"Well, you need to get used to it." She rubbed her mouth with the back of her hand, but it did little to diminish the hot taste of him. "I'm marrying Rupert."

"We'll see." He stomped away from her.

"Yes, we will!" she yelled at his retreating form.

Chapter Four

Elle sat at a table in the diner, alone, trying to gather her wits. Her lips still tingled from the brutal yet sensual kiss Graham had bestowed upon her. His slate-colored eyes glowed with arousal while desire laced her blood and need pounded through her veins. Rupert didn't kiss her in such a way. Not even close.

Picking up her fork to eat her Cobb salad, she went over what she planned to say to Drew. He could trust Rupert. His father was a good senator. His family was very...conservative. She frowned. She wasn't campaigning for them. She only wanted Drew to give her fiancé a chance and allow him onto pack lands. They'd travel back to North Carolina for visits.

Drew is going to love him and his conservative values. Why don't you say he's also a gun toting member of the NRA while you're at it?

She pushed her food away, her stomach roiling with guilt.

Her phone rang.

She pulled her cell out of her pocket. Kizzy's image grinned from the screen. Elle sighed. Leaving her life in North Carolina behind wouldn't be as easy as Shawn said. She tapped the screen to open the text message.

Me again. Are you sure you're okay? You didn't sound okay. If you need me.... ~K2E2

Her best friend since she moved to Charlotte, Kizzy had a kind spirit and a penchant for all things geeky. She lived and breathed *Star Wars*, and when she realized their initials could form a cute homage to R2D2, she signed everything with it. Leaving her behind

had been hard. She loved her friend dearly, but Elle knew the rules—
no one could know about Los Lobos or the Tao Pack.

Really, I'm fine. If I need you, I will call. ~E

She paid her bill and left the diner. So much had changed since
she'd fled Los Lobos. Everyone appeared, happy. An air of freedom
surrounded her pack mates as they meandered around town. Such a
stark contrast to when Magnum had been alpha. She didn't scent
their fears or heartache. This, she could get used to. She could see
herself spending the rest of her life in Los Lobos. She had a purpose,
now, as she strolled through town. In order for her life to be
complete, she had to shore up the finer details.

As she stepped up onto her alpha's porch, the door opened and
Betty greeted her. "Welcome home, Elle." She wrapped her in a hug.
The warmth of the embrace had Elle smiling. "I'm so glad you made
it and the rumors weren't true. Come on in."

She followed Betty to Drew's office. The door stood ajar. Inside,
Drew sat behind a handcrafted oak desk. To his right stood the man
who'd saved her life. Ryker. His imposing figure filled the room. A
shiver of dread slithered down her spine just as it had the night he
sent her away. The urge to run consumed her.

Then.... *Oh my God.* One corner of his mouth twitched. *Is
he...smiling?* She looked away, not sure of what she'd just seen.

Laughing slightly, Betty guided her forward. "Yes, things have
changed since you've been gone."

Elle stood before her alpha and his enforcer, gaze cast toward
the floor.

"You know, when Ryker told me he saved you, I thought he was
full of shit. I guess I owe him twenty dollars." The chair Drew sat in
squeaked. "Welcome home, Elle St. Claire. You're allowed to look at
me."

When she raised her gaze, Drew gifted her with a brilliant,
comforting smile. "Thank you, Alpha. It's good to be home."

"It's Drew. Have a seat." He pointed to the chair next to her.
Once she sat, he said, "Have you considered what kind of job you'd
like, since you've returned. I know you've only been here a couple of
days, but it never hurts to contemplate what's next."

Back in Charlotte, she'd been a receptionist for a prestigious
clinical psychologist. He worked with movie stars and with some of
the state legislature's spouses. But how could she transfer those
skills here? Last she saw, everyone had normal, hardworking jobs.

No one sat on their ass in an office, talking about their anxiety or which star cheated on their spouse with another actor. "No. I hadn't considered the possibility of finding anything here."

"What do you do in Charlotte?"

"I'm a receptionist for a prominent psychologist. I schedule all the appointments, fetch lunch when need be...you know, all the glamorous things a receptionist does for her boss."

"Hmm." Drew tapped his chin. "Do you like your job?"

"Yes." She grinned. She loved seeing the transformation clients went through from the time they first arrived, broken and beaten down, to the self-confidence they exuded by their last session. She also liked the celebrity gossip she'd overhear. Some days, it made the hours fly by. "It's rewarding and gives me a sense of purpose."

He picked up his phone off the table and hit a few buttons then held it to his ear. "Brie," he said, his gaze locking with Elle's. "I'm good. So is B. I have a question for you." He smiled and gave a short chuckle. "I have a wolf here who needs a job, and I know you could use an assistant. Would you mind talking to her? Great...great. I'll send her to you. Her name is Elle St. Claire."

After a few more pleasantries, he ended the call. "Brienne Talbort-Blu could use an assistant, as you heard. She is working with the abused wolves of the pack. She is a licensed therapist. I think you'll like her."

"Really?"

He nodded. "She has a fifteen-minute window before her next client. If you're willing to head over there now."

Shocked, she didn't know what to do. "Yes," flew from her mouth, and before she could say, "Wait, what about Rupert?" Betty whisked her away, giving her directions on how to find Brie's office on the way out the door. Her mind tried to process what happened. She had a job—even though she'd thought about quitting the one she had in Charlotte to become a full-time housewife, since kids were in the cards for her and Rupert. He came from a huge family, so, naturally, they'd have many as well. Her wolf sneered at the thought.

"You look a little lost." Shawn stepped out of his office.

"I think I've lost everything," she muttered. "How did this happen?"

"Brie called me, said you might be headed her way. Want a lift?" He hooked his thumb at his truck. "It'll give you time to absorb everything."

"Thanks. I appreciate it."

He led her to his truck, opening the door for her. "Climb on in." After he closed her door, he took his spot behind the wheel and pulled away from the curb, heading away from town. "What happened?"

"I'm not sure. I had a plan in mind on how this would all work out. But now...I don't know." She fiddled with the ring on her finger, the weight of it a reminder of her responsibility.

"It's a lot to take in. Maybe you should go for a run. Clear your mind."

A run sounded fabulous. Her wolf brushed against her skin, eager to get out. "Maybe."

"You're not going to do it, are you?"

"It's complicated. I have a list of things to do before I can relax and be a wolf. When I am done and things are prepared properly, I'll give in to my baser needs." Her wolf snorted.

"When did you last run?"

The question, though simple enough, left her speechless. She couldn't remember the last time she'd let the wolf out. "I'm not sure."

"I'm giving you a piece of advice." He shot her a side glance. "Whether you want it or not. Fuck the planning bullshit. You're a wolf, not a human. Your wolf has wants and desires, something it sounds like you've been denying for a long time. You're free here. You don't have to hide anymore."

Each word hit her like a hammer, pounding home a truth she wasn't sure she wanted to hear. "I'll give it some thought," she said, as he pulled up to a newly built home. The woman she supposed was Brie stood on the porch waiting. "I better go."

Shawn growled. "She's a good woman, and my mate. Don't do anything stupid to hurt her because you can't figure out what you're supposed to do."

Elle frowned. "I'd never."

"Good. Keep it that way."

She exited the truck then walked up the stairs.

Brie extended her hand. The auburn-haired woman gave her a welcoming smile. "Don't worry about him. He's a little overprotective of me."

"Yeah, I could tell." She followed her inside the house and glanced around. *Whoa. Mellow.*

The walls were painted in soft, relaxing shades of butter and cream. The furnishings invoked a feeling of comfort and hominess. She trailed the woman back to a small office space, again done in neutral tones. Behind the desk, hanging on the wall were two degrees. Next to them sat a small bookcase with several journals and medical guides. A couple of framed college awards were scattered among knickknacks, while a picture of Brie and Shawn sat on another shelf.

"Drew tells me you were an assistant back in Charlotte." She took her seat behind the desk.

"Yes. I loved—*love* my job."

"Good. I need someone who is self-motivated, can work under pressure, and isn't afraid to get her hands dirty."

"Can do." Elle glanced around. The house didn't seem all that big. "But where would I be working? Isn't this your home?"

Brie laughed. "No. This is my office. There is a room directly next to my office where I do the sessions and one more on the opposite side for you. The space up front is the waiting room, and, yes, I have a small but efficient kitchen for coffee and snacks."

She blinked. Then blinked again. "Forgive me, but why did you put your office all the way out here?" The forest surrounded the building. On the way here, she'd noticed no other houses.

"Because sometimes the quietest places are the easiest places to heal. Our pack mates come here to deal with the devastation left behind by a cruel alpha. They need the serenity and peace seclusion can give them. And, when they need to be a wolf, they can go out the back door and run."

Wow.

Brie smiled. "So, do you want the job?"

How could she say no? The thought of not being here with Brie didn't even enter her mind. Nor had the doubts she'd had while meeting with Drew. "When do I start?"

Chapter Five

Two days after he'd seen Elle in town, Graham sat astride his horse, trying to figure shit out. The kiss had knocked him for a loop. He hadn't realized how much he wanted her until she pushed off of him, leading him to walk away. He couldn't force this, nor would he. She needed to come to him of her own free will.

Watching the bees dance in the wind while landing on small flowers, he remembered a time when she'd been just as carefree. He missed her laughter. Her smile. He missed the way she placed her hand on the middle of his chest then buried her face in the crook of his neck—

Kalum smacked his leg.

"What?"

"I said you seem awfully distracted." His brother stood beside him. "Want to talk about it?"

No. "I'm not sure where to begin."

"Why don't you start from the beginning?"

Graham stared out over the pastureland. *The beginning. Boy, no pressure there.* "I saw Elle in town two days ago. I kind of was a prick."

Kal grinned and smacked his leg again. "At some point, we all are. We're dominant wolves. It's just our nature."

"Yeah, well…. I think I pushed her away more than brought her to me." He rubbed the back of his neck. "I kissed her."

His brother narrowed his eyes. "Okay, why is that a bad thing?"

Not like his courtship with Fawn had been any easier. Every time his brother approached the timid little wolf, she'd tucked tail and given some excuse or another why they shouldn't go on a simple date. It had taken an elaborate scheme to get her to at least consider something more with Kalum.

"In the past few days, the urge to find my mate has ridden me so damn hard I almost can't take it. I feel like, any minute, I might go feral. She's avoiding me. Showing off that fucking diamond on her finger, like if she shows it more, it'll make it right," he grumbled. "Then I kissed her. Everything on my end slid into place. I walked away, though. I didn't want to hear again how wrong it is and how happy she is."

"It's natural. She's afraid, and rightfully so. We don't know what happened that night, but maybe you should ask. It might help figure this shit out between the two of you."

"I don't know." It was why he sat there, staring at nothing, trying to put his thoughts into some kind of cohesive order.

His brother whistled. "Man, for once I'm glad I have Fawn. I don't have to worry about this bullshit anymore." He scrubbed his jaw. "Just going to throw this out there. Have you ever thought about telling her how you feel?"

Graham snorted. "I did."

"And?"

"And nothing."

"Then the question becomes, are you running because you're pissed off about some ring, or are you running off because you're not ready?"

"Probably both," Graham replied. "I'm not sure how to fix it, though."

"Well, you can begin by stop being such a morose asshole, and start talking to people. You have a house full of women who know how a woman's mind works. Then you need to set something up for the both of you, like a place to live after your mating. Finally, don't give her a way out."

He considered his brother's advice and nodded. "I think that might work." Already, ideas began to take form in his mind. Now, all he had to do was find Elle.

"Good. So can we stop acting like a bunch of clucking hens and start pushing some cows?"

Graham nodded. "Let's do it. Yah!" He snapped the reins in his hand, and his horse took off.

The whole time they pushed the cattle, Graham did nothing but think about what Kal had suggested. Since he'd seen Elle in town, memories of their time together filled his mind. Maybe he'd set up a picnic for them. The pasturelands held some secluded spots even the cows didn't go. He could take her out there. Ask her what happened. Really listen to her. *Mate her.* If she was responsive to it. But it could wait.

After he put up his horse and got cleaned up, he found Fawn sitting in her usual spot, reading. She'd promised Kal she'd only work in the mornings then relax the rest of the day. Her belly swelled with their pup. If this all worked out, would Elle want kids, too? Could he be a dad? Did he want to?

"Hey." She looked up from her book. "Are you guys done for the day?"

"Pretty much. Can we talk for a second?"

"Sure. I was wondering when we'd get a chance with all the changes going on around here. I heard about your kiss with Elle in town."

"Yeah, about that." He approached the couch where she sat. Since she'd moved in with them, little changes had occurred. Knickknacks. More of those nature ornaments Kalum bought her for Christmas. Her collection of mugs not only filled the office Kalum had made for her, but also lined the kitchen cupboards. "I didn't expect to be so assholish an—"

"How long have you known?"

"Ten years." He sat forward, his elbows on his knees. "But I thought she died. I should have died. I don't understand." Yet, a piece of him had always felt her. Always known she'd survived. Though, at the time, he'd thought it wishful thinking.

"Why didn't you tell someone? We would have helped you deal with your grief, or something." The absolute conviction in her voice astounded him.

"When? It didn't feel right with you and Kalum settling in then everything with Kru coming home and Gabby. Hell, I have a sister who is fighting her attraction to mine and Kal's best friend because who knows why." He blew out a breath of frustration. "Add in the murders plus you and Gabby being pregnant, and I couldn't ask anyone to do anything."

"So you decided to struggle through this on your own?"

He shrugged.

"Stubborn ass." She rubbed her belly. "So, what can I do for you?"

"I don't know. She keeps running from me. I just want to fix this. I want my mate."

"If I tell you what to do, will you do it?"

He met her gaze. "You have my word."

"Then I'll tell you everything I can to help you out." She set her book on the small table next to the couch.

"Thank you, Fawn. I owe you."

She laughed. "Don't thank me yet."

***

Graham stepped inside The Den to grab Fawn a burger. For almost an hour, she'd given him tip after tip. Things he hadn't thought of. Don't push too hard. Be compassionate. Ask her about her life then back off. Let her come to him. As much as his wolf may protest, he had to allow Elle to be the one to make the next move.

Heading for the bar, he pulled up short when he spotted the object of his lust-filled thoughts. By herself, Elle sat in a booth. The ring on her finger tore at his gut and pissed him off, but if he meant to win her over, he needed to swallow the rage and embrace the ability to see her.

Strolling to her, he stopped at the edge of the table and waited for her to acknowledge him. When she didn't, he cleared his throat. She glanced up at him and blanched. Her clean, sweet-wheat scent wafted up to him. The light, mouth-watering tendrils of her arousal wrapped around him. Determination built inside him. He'd coax the sugary aroma from her just so he could bask in it.

"Can I join you?" He pointed to the seat across from her.

Her gaze shifted between him and the bench, and then, like a deer caught in the headlights of an oncoming car, she stared at him.

"It's not a hard question, honey."

She opened her mouth. Closed it then tried again. "I suppose so."

"Thanks."

She eyed him warily as he sat.

"Have you ordered yet?"

"No." She set the menu on the table. "You'd think I'd remember all Gee serves is burgers, fried pickles, and broccoli."

Graham laughed. "He makes a few other things, if you ask

nicely. Want to share a plate of loaded fries?"

"What the heck. You only live once, right?"

"Exactly." He waved Paul over and gave their order. When he retreated to the kitchen, Graham spoke again. "I need to apologize."

She pulled the plump flesh of her bottom lip between her teeth, and he growled. The pink tinge covering her cheeks along with the way her breath hitched had his groin tightening. "For what?"

"My outburst. I'm a frustrated wolf. I'm hurting."

Her gaze softened, her body relaxed. "I'm sorry."

"Don't be. You did nothing wrong. You got out, as did we. After years of believing you dead...I'm happy you're alive."

"I wouldn't have if it weren't for Ryker. He deserves your thanks."

Graham leaned in, his fingertips grazing the back of her hand. "What happened? We could smell everything and see the smoke from the fire. How did he get you out?"

"Greer wanted what he couldn't have," she said, her words barely above a whisper. "Said it was his duty to break in the fertile females of the pack."

Greer. Rage burned in his gut. *The fucking weasel. Slithering through the pack like a little broke-back bitch, doing the bidding of his demonized alpha.* He swallowed the need to kill, knowing Elle would be able to sense the anger building in him. This wasn't about him. It was her story.

Are you okay, Elle?

"She's okay, Paul. Thank you." He smiled at the omega. Since finding PG, his mate, the man had really come out of his shell. Could talk their ears off, given half a chance, since the majority of them were learning sign language, including Graham.

He nodded. *If you need anything, ask.*

Once Paul moved out of earshot, Graham prompted her to continue. "It's okay. You're safe."

She took a deep breath then let it out slowly. "The day Greer came for me was my mother's birthday. I planned on making her something pretty. She loved pressed flowers and I needed another, smaller bunch. I already had the wax paper and the iron set out, waiting for me. All of the flowers were in bloom. I didn't know which ones to choose because Mom would love all of them. So I decided to pick as many as I could carry. I had extra paper and could make the project a little bigger." She pushed a lock of hair behind her ear. "I smelled the smoke first, about halfway home. Saw the fire when I topped the hill. I started running for the house, but...." She took a deep breath. Her bottom lip trembled. "Ryker was there. I'm not sure where he came from. He told me my parents were dead and to run and not stop until I got to Hill City. The fierceness in his gaze kept me from saying anything or demanding answers. So, I ran."

His wolf howled in agony. Sliding across the seat, he had to be closer to her. Graham wrapped his arm around her, pressing her face to his neck while rubbing her back. The soft sobs emanating from her tore at his heart. "You would have been killed if you stayed."

"I know...now." She sniffed.

"I'm glad you ran." He caressed her tear-stained cheek. "I thought I'd die without you." He tipped her chin up and brushed his lips over hers. Be damned her ring and her human fiancé. The need to show her—to claim her—rushed through him.

Elle shifted her position, pressing them closer together. He deepened the kiss, slanting his mouth over hers, so they were better fused. She stoked a fire in him—one long dormant, that had settled to soft glowing embers—and she, like a whip of oxygen, breathed life back into him. Without her, he didn't exist.

"Graham," she murmured as she laid her head to his shoulder.

"I've got you. You're safe now."

The thread connecting them as children snapped into place, stronger, better. The stiffness in her form eased as she melded into him and he reveled in it. Now he had her, he wouldn't let her go.

All those nights he'd lain awake, wondering about her, what it would've been like to build a life with her. Wishing she'd lived.... He frowned. "The hardest day of my life was when Magnum announced that you and your family died in the fire. There were three bodies—"

She looked up at him. "Three?"

He nodded. "Little to nothing was left. But, because there were three, I had no choice but to believe what they said. You were gone. No one questioned it." He held her tighter. "But you escaped. You lived."

"I wonder who—"

The jingle of a ringtone broke through the cocoon surrounding them.

She closed her eyes. "Sorry." After rifling through her bag, she pulled out her phone and sighed. "I have to answer this." She hit the talk button. "Hello?" Her brow furrowed. "Wait, slow down, Kizzy. You're where?"

He heard every bit of the conversation, thanks to his wolf hearing.

"I'm in Hill City." The frantic tone in her friend's voice grew as the seconds pushed on. "Are you in trouble?"

"I'm fine," Elle assured her. "What do you mean you're in Hill City?"

"After our last conversation, something didn't ring right. I had to come see you, so I followed you."

Resourceful girl. He'd chuckle if he weren't so pissed.

"I have stuff I need to take care of," Elle snapped. "I'm fine. Leave it alone."

"Well, I'm in Hill City, but you're not here."

"God, Kizzy. Why did you follow me?" Tension filled his mate. Whoever this Kizzy person was, Elle liked her, even if the girl drove her insane.

"Look, you'd been sneaking around for days. That's not you. So, I trailed you to the bus station, figured out where you were headed. At first I thought, let you do your thing, you'd share later. But then there was that note about needing to see your mom, but I know she's dead, and even after we talked on the phone.... I don't know. I got worried. Can we talk about this face-to-face?"

Elle's shoulders slumped. "I don't know. It's...complicated."

"I'm at the Hill City Inn."

Shit. The girl is insane. He pulled his phone out and sent a quick message to Drew, seeking a meeting. When he received a quick response for first thing in the morning, he agreed. At the same moment he put his phone away, she did the same. "We'll go see her tomorrow. Don't worry."

She brushed off his comment. "She means well. She's kind and geeky. I'm about her only friend due to her quirkiness." She grabbed a fry off the plate, popped it into her mouth then moaned. "So good. Thank you." She gifted him a small smile, even after recalling the night of her parents' deaths, and her best friend's phone call.

His heart gave a heavy thump. His gut clenched. If buying her loaded fries brought even a tiny bit of joy to her life, he'd do it every day. "You don't have to thank me, honey. It's my pleasure."

Chapter Six

E lle stared up at the Hill City diner sign. Somewhere inside sat Kizzy. The girl, though a little bit of a pain in the ass, meant the world to her. She glanced at Graham who wore a weary expression. It'd seemed so simple when she stepped off the bus a few days ago. She had a plan, and needed to stick to it, yet the more time she spent in the hills, the less she wanted to go back to North Carolina. The less she wanted to see Rupert.

In the beginning, she thought she knew what she wanted, but now...not so much. Her wolf, on the other hand, wanted the man beside her. She'd known her mate all those years ago, but time had gotten in the way of things. Muddling everything. And, what would she say to Rupert? *Sorry, but I found the real guy I'm supposed to be with. Here's your ring back. Good luck becoming a senator?*

Ugh, why did it have to be so dang hard? Why couldn't she say yes to Graham and the hell to everything else? Why did she have to have a knot of guilt in her stomach whenever she thought of Rupert?

"Ready to find your friend?" Graham's soft tone drew her out of her self-recriminating thoughts.

"Yeah, I think so. She's different, okay? Be nice to her." She had quirks and a unique perspective on life. Sometimes people enjoyed her, and sometimes people made fun of her.

"You sound like a nervous mother," he teased.

"I feel like it." They opened the door and stepped inside the diner. Behind the counter, a woman poured coffee into a customer's cup while chatting with another person.

"There you are." Kizzy pulled Elle into an embrace. "I worried so much about you."

"I'm fine." She grunted, trying to breathe through the bone-crushing hug. "See? Nothing to be worried about." She allowed Kizzy to guide them back to her table situated by the door. "How are you?"

She narrowed her eyes, pushing her cat-eye glasses up on her nose. She wore a Dr. Who T-Shirt, and her hair had been pulled back into a severe ponytail. Her skinny jeans were complemented by a pair of low-rise Chuck Taylors, blue, like the Tardis. "Who are you?" She looked to Elle as they sat at a table near the windows. "Who is this? He's hot in a predator kinda way. Big...rangy." She eyed him up and down. "I like him."

Graham cocked a brow.

"Kizzy, this is Graham. My...friend." She smiled.

"You look more like a Beau or a Wyatt." She turned her attention back to Elle. "Where did you find a cowboy?"

"Well, we are in South Dakota...so, they happen to roam around here."

"Cool." Her friend nodded. "Why are you here? The truth this time."

Oh God, she's had candy. "Okay, chick-a-dee, where's your stash?"

Her eyebrows shot up over the tops of her glasses. "I'll have you know I haven't had any candy. I had a couple of cups of fancy coffee. No, scratch that. Could have been a double espresso or two. I had to keep my mind occupied while you were off gallivanting around the countryside with this stud muffin." She hooked her thumb at him.

Elle groaned, chancing a peek at Graham. He looked absolutely bewildered. "Oh God. Kizzy, I'm fine. I'm happy here."

"Great." She smacked the table then took a sip of her water. "But *why* are you here?"

"It's complicated. The easy answer is this is where I'm from. I came home. I needed time away. To clear my head." She twisted the ring on her finger and licked her lips. "We work so hard. You know."

"Bullshit." Kizzy laughed. "You couldn't wait to get the hell out of town. You didn't even tell Rupert. Just left him that note. I need the truth."

"The truth is...complicated. You should know I am safe, though. No one is keeping me against my will. No one threatened me. I'm happy." She took her friend's hand. "Promise me you won't tell anyone about where I am."

She waved Elle off. "Not even an issue."

Breathing a sigh of relief, she grabbed a menu. "How long are you going to stay?"

"Well, I hadn't thought about it. I was more concerned about you." She glanced around the diner. "I can see why you like this place. It's open and moves at a slower pace."

She nodded. "I agree."

"What about Rupert?"

She didn't have an answer for her. "I'm here to figure it out."

Kizzy squealed. "You mean it?"

"Um, yes?"

"Fantastic!"

Graham laughed. The deep, rich rumble warmed her while it vibrated across her skin, leaving goose bumps in its wake.

"Damn, that's sexy."

"Oh my God, Kizzy! Be good, jeez." She sighed, shaking her head. If she meant to embarrass Elle, she'd done a good job of it so far.

She reached up, adjusted her glasses. "I'll try."

The waitress came to the table. "Can I take your order?"

Kizzy pointed to the menu. "Rocky Mountain Oysters. Really?" She cocked a brow. "Poor bulls."

Graham choked. "We'll have burgers and fries and a piece of your pie of the day."

"It's lemon meringue." The waitress wrote down their order.

"Fine."

"Anything else?" She held her pen, poised to write down whatever else they ordered.

"No. Maybe, when we leave, we'll have a to-go order for you." He smiled.

After the waitress walked away, Kizzy eased forward. "When you're ready to go home, I'll go with you."

How did she explain to her friend she didn't intend to return to North Carolina? "Uh, sure."

"Great. So, what are we doing today?"

"I thought we could hang out." She shrugged.

"Okay. Not going to show me where you're staying?"

Shit. She'd known her friend would ask too many question. "Nope. Not right now. I'm staying with friends, and the house is full. But I'm safe there. Like I said before I left, my life is complicated. I need to fix a few things then my life will be better."

Kizzy side eyed her. "I don't like that answer. You've always been evasive about this part of your life. I just wish I understood."

"I know. I'm sorry. I wish I could explain." *Please drop it. Please don't ask me any more questions.*

"You know, they have a shootout here at noon." Graham's interjection caught her best friend's attention.

"Seriously?"

"Yeah." He glanced up at the neon clock on the wall. "In about thirty minutes. If we can eat soon, maybe we can get out there and watch." Thank God for small favors.

"You're trying to bamboozle me."

He smirked. "And here I thought you'd like to explore town with us."

Her friend let out a huff. "Fine. We'll discuss this later."

Not if I can help it. "Sure." The waitress arrived just in the nick of time with their food. "Eat up. We have a whole day planned with you."

Four hours later, after they'd spent the day with Kizzy, Graham turned onto the dirt road heading for Kalum's house. Elle didn't like lying to her friend. She didn't like secrets, but not telling her was a matter of protecting the pack. The pack came first. While she was in Charlotte, she didn't have to worry about the dynamic. The only thing she hid was her true nature.

As they pulled into the driveway, Ryker stepped out from the woods. Somehow, she'd had a feeling he'd be crossing her path again. The connection they shared—hero and rescuee—bonded them together.

Graham stopped and shut off the truck, and she got out. "Hi."

"Drew sent me," Ryker stated.

"Ah." Elle stared up at the pack enforcer. "Why?"

"To explain. About the night—"

"My parents died."

He nodded.

"How much did you know about what would happen?" She needed to know the truth. None of it, even today, felt real.

He grunted. "Your parents planned your escape."

Her heart squeezed. Tears blurred her eyes. "I should have known."

"I believe they wanted the best for you. They put the money aside for several months and enlisted my help you get away.

She nodded. Her wolf howled in pain. In those last hours with her family, her father had been providing a way for her. She'd never truly been alone.

"Gee went to Hill City, left the money for you but didn't buy the ticket. You had to choose your destiny. East or west, he knew you would be safe."

"Sounds like Gee." She nodded. "But why didn't my parents go with me?"

"They wanted you safe first." His jaw tightened. "They'd planned to follow, but Greer arrived early."

"He killed my parents." Her heart ached with loss just as it had the day she'd run toward her burning home. She wiped her eyes. "Where is Greer now?"

"Dead."

She shoved her hands in her pockets, the truth, after all these years, finally clear. "He's the third body." Things hadn't gone the way her parents had planned. Ryker had done his best to carry out their wishes to keep her safe, making it look like she'd died, too, by throwing Greer's body in the fire. Made sense. "Never mind, rhetorical question. But didn't Magnum ask about Greer?"

He shrugged.

Apparently, he'd found a way around it. *Obviously, since Ryker didn't die that night as well.* "Thank you."

"You're welcome." He unnerved her once again with a smirk.

"But how did you know where I was?"

"I have my ways."

"Should have figured as much." She scrunched up her nose. "But why now?"

He shrugged. "You're home."

Simple enough. "Thanks. You know, for everything."

He inclined his head. "Don't tell your friend about us."

She gasped. "How did you know?"

"I know. The rules are in place to protect us. Even if you trust her, a slip of the tongue is all it takes to bring us down." He strode off as if their conversation never happened.

"I won't tell," she called out. "Promise."

Chapter Seven

Kathy and the other matrons sat at their usual spot inside The Den. When their food arrived, she ate in silence, her mind on the issues with their latest match.

"I can't take it anymore. Shouldn't that fiancé of Elle's have called by now?" She tapped her fingers against the table. *Graham and Elle aren't finishing things. They should be mated by now.* "Something isn't right."

"Surely if the man loves her enough to want to marry her, he'd be worried?" Claire agreed.

"My Henry wouldn't let me out of his sight for even an hour when we were first mated. This man should be searching for her." Fern fingered the necklace around her neck. "Her friend called, though. Kizzy, I think her name is." She leaned in. "From what I've heard, she's hell on wheels and would give any wolf a run."

"We're not here to make a match, ladies." Anger burned in her guts. "Elle's fiancé should be looking for her and I'm going to find out why he's not." She stood. "I'll be back."

She stepped outside into the midday sun and sighed. Something wasn't right with that man. How could Elle run away so easily without so much as a peep from her fiancé? Clyde would have broken down doors and killed to find her. She thought about the human aspect of it, and, though they seemed a little different within the pack, the love she saw in each of the human mate's eyes spoke volumes. They, like their wolf counterparts, would kill to protect what was theirs. She strolled down the sidewalk, turning the information over in her mind, until she stood in front of Shawn's office. What she'd thought would be a quick walk to clear her mind and gather her thoughts seemed to lead her exactly where she needed to be.

Kathy opened the door to the office and stepped inside. Shawn sat at his desk, going over something on his computer. The man had been working hard to bring home more of their pack. It seemed every week now one or two made their way into town and back into their families. She sat in the chair across from him and rapped her knuckles on the table.

He glanced up from his work and smirked. "I knew you were there. I wondered how long you'd let me ignore you is all."

"Pups," she huffed. "I need your help."

"Anything." He grabbed a pad. "What's the problem?"

"The problem is, that good for nothing fiancé hasn't said spit to Elle since she left." Kathy crossed her arms. "Don't you find it strange?"

"I mean...I guess I do. Are you sure they're even together anymore?" He glanced up from his pad.

"Yes. Gee explained as much after he saw her at the gutted remains of her place."

"Hmm. Interesting. What do you need me to do?"

"Isn't it obvious, boy? I want you to go to Charlotte and find out what he's doing. My guess is, he has a little dove on the side." A hunch was all she had, but a hunch would do in a pinch. If it were true, then she could present it to Elle, and it'd be the kick in the ass the couple needed.

"I have a better idea. I have a contact already there. I'll put him on the job and tell him we need a rush on it. Sound like a plan?"

She nodded. "Don't take too long."

"I won't," he assured her. "Anything else?"

"No, not off the top of my head. But, if I think of something, I'll be back."

Shawn grinned. "I'll be waiting with bated breath for your return."

"Don't be a smart ass, boy." She chuckled.

"Blame Henry. I get it from him."

"I'll bet you do," she muttered, leaving his business. Once she was outside, she set off back to The Den.

The ruckus of Gee's bar greeted her a few steps from the old wooden building. Along the side, couples in all manner of entanglements, groped and kissed, the scent of mating heavy in the air. *To be young again.* To have the freeness of a willing partner who didn't give a shit where they took you, as long as it was hard and fast and left you wrung out like a wet noodle. Maybe she'd kick Clyde into gear.

Inside, the ladies were laughing. She took her seat then gulped down the rest of her drink. "What did I miss?"

"Nothing much," Lonnie replied. "We're talking about new matches."

"A specific boy," Claire added.

"Oh? Do tell."

"Sayer." Fern grinned.

"The wolf with a surly attitude?" The protector had a mean streak a mile long. She couldn't blame him. Being forced to watch your parents die because they made the mistake of helping humans—who'd eventually been killed as well—didn't bode well for a child's psyche.

"Yes!" Claire looked positively excited.

A knot of trepidation filled her. "What are you planning?"

"Nothing much," Fern answered. "Setting up contingency plans."

"Shit."

"I said the same," Lonnie groused.

"Relax." Fern patted her hand. "Everything is going to work out perfectly."

***

A knock came at the door while Elle read from one of Miss Kathy's Orion Davis books. She loved all the paranormal and science fiction novels Kizzy kept at her home. Loved the movies she had tucked away in the cabinets near her television. She dog-eared the page and stood as the knock came again.

Taking a tentative step toward the door, she stopped and fisted her hands. "Who's there?"

"Elle." Graham's drawl surprised her. "Open up."

She closed the distance between her and the door then pulled it open. "What are you doing here?"

"Can I come in? I wanted to talk to you."

She bit her bottom lip and glanced over her shoulder at her temporary home. "Sure." She stepped aside.

He walked in, removing his hat while he did. "I know everything has been messed up. But I can't get you out of my mind."

She knew she'd have to face her feelings sooner or later. She missed him. She wanted him. She was scared. Afraid of what would be said about her. Afraid of—and it was ridiculous to think such—what would happen to Rupert. Yet, for all the gumption in the world, she couldn't quite find a reason not to pursue this track in her life. Though she had worries, and a little guilt, it didn't hold back what she knew. The man standing in front of her was and would always be, her mate. "I can't stop thinking about you either."

He leaned in and nuzzled her neck. "I'm sorry." He pressed his lips to her skin. "I should have never stopped looking for you. I should have done more."

Elle shook her head, stepping out of his embrace. "You would have been killed. Greer, through Magnum's vicious pull, went insane. He wanted the blood. He wanted death. He wanted me."

He stalked toward her, determination filled his eyes. "I can't even think about that night." He pulled her into his arms again. "All I smelled was burning flesh and wood. The miasma of death. My wolf raged. He howled for you. Cried for you as I did. I mourned you every day. But I felt you. I thought…." He tightened his embrace. "I thought, because there were three bodies, I must be feeling your spirit. You know, so, in my head, it made sense."

"But the body wasn't me. It was Greer."

He nodded. "I know that now. But at the time, I thought you were trying to tell me to move on, to find another. But every time I looked, none of them compared to you. None of them held a candle to your kindness. Your sweetness. Your tender soul. I thought for sure I'd gone insane. Was ready to leave because, if I did lose it, I didn't want to be near anyone I could hurt. Then Shawn called me, and I saw you." He nipped at the side of her throat, sending tingles of electricity through her.

She closed her eyes and bit the inside of her cheek to keep from asking for more.

"I've missed you every day."

"I wanted to tell you," she whimpered. "Several times in the last few years, I wanted to come home. But Ryker told me never to return." Once the fountain of truth had been opened, she couldn't close it. "And, even then, I wanted to find you, to be with you. But I got scared."

He tipped her chin up and crushed her lips with his. He explored her. The kiss was slow, building with intensity each time he stroked his tongue against hers. He caressed her hips, pushing the billowy material of her shirt out of the way. "We're together now. You never have to be afraid again."

"What are your expectations?" Her heart pounded. Her girly parts tingled with arousal, while her soul hoped he'd say the words she longed to hear.

"Isn't it obvious?"

"Kind of, but I'd like to hear the words." She tentatively ran her hands over his chest.

"I'm finishing what we started ten years ago." He bit her ear lobe. "I'm making you mine." His hand fisted her hair. "Got any objections to my plan?"

She gasped, and her eyes fluttered shut. "Only a request," she squeaked.

"Shoot."

"Miss Kathy and Clyde will be home soon." His mouth returned to her neck, kissing a path down to her collarbone. "I don't think it's appropriate for them to see us naked."

Graham chuckled. "No, they don't need to see us naked." He ground his groin into her lower belly. "Anything else?"

"Yes."

"Oh?"

"Never leave me alone again," she replied.

"That's a given, beautiful." He gazed down at her. Desire blazed in his eyes. "My place is at your side."

Elle stepped around him then held out her hand. "My bedroom is this way."

Graham placed his hand in hers. "Are you sure?"

She couldn't deny her destiny any longer. "Yes."

His eyes filled with possessiveness. "Lead the way."

Chapter Eight

Were they really going to do this? Elle squeezed Graham's hand, pulling him to a stop. "You should know, I've only had one partner. Rupert."

A slow, sensual grin spread across his lips. "I've had a few but nothing serious."

"Seriously?"

He let out a breath of frustration. "I know I have tons of explaining to do after we're settled. But no. Though I had moments of needing that physical connection, I never formed any kind of bond with them. I knew, the moment I held you in my arms, I'd wait for you."

Her heart lodged in her throat. Tears threatened to spill down her cheeks. *Is he for real?* "Now you're just looking for brownie points.

His bark of laughter startled her. "Beautiful, you've got no idea the lengths I'd go to stay in your good graces."

She smiled a little. "Then what are we waiting for?" She pushed the door open then glanced down at her finger, the weight of the rock an inconvenience. She slipped it off, and the moment it left her hand, the world seemed brighter, freer. She stepped inside her temporary room, Graham trailing behind her, and she placed it in her bag. She then crossed the room and sat on the bed covered in buckskin blankets and soft quilts and held her hand out to her mate.

"I'm tired of waiting." He yanked at his shirt, the snaps flying apart in rapid succession. "Before we get started, are you—"

She covered his mouth with her hand. "I am. Even though a child wouldn't be a bad thing, I think we should take our time."

He covered her mouth again with his. A ferocious hunger the likes of which she never experienced overtook her. Her fingers fumbled with the button of his jeans while he feasted on her. Her hands trembled. Anxious energy raced through her. She was ready to begin the next phase in her life, one she'd begun many years ago, only to be thwarted by time and circumstance. *Not today.* Today she'd become the person she'd meant to be. With a growl of frustration, Graham laid his hands on top of hers, steadying her.

"Easy, beautiful. We've got all the time in the world." His fingers skimmed up her sides as he pulled her blouse off. "Fucking perfect." He dipped his head and latched onto her nipple through the see-through lace of her bra.

Elle arched her back, and clung to him for support as pleasure zinged through her. A cry of need fell from her lips when he switched to her other breast and administered the same attention. His slate-blue eyes locked with hers with each suck. Her pussy ached; her clit throbbed. The thought occurred to her, they weren't the fumbling kids they used to be. They were older, taking their time to enjoy the experience. He trailed kisses across her chest as he worked her pants from her hips then down her legs.

She ran her fingers through his hair, eliciting a moan from him. His hips flexed and the thick press of his denim-clad erection slid across her exposed flesh. "Elle," he murmured.

He hovered over her, taking his fill of her once more before pressing his lips between her breasts. He kissed a path down her belly, paying special attention to her navel. He nibbled at the edges then dipped his tongue inside. She wiggled beneath him, grasped at his biceps for purchase. If he meant to make her suffer, he was doing a spectacular job of it. Her body came to life, heating to the point she feared she'd combust.

"Graham," she whimpered, raising her hips in invitation.

"Soon." He teased the band of her panties with his fingertips. Then took his time exposing her flesh to his perusal. "Mine!" He nuzzled her mons then ran his tongue over her slit. "The sweetest treat a man could ever have." He placed a kiss to both of her thighs. "I've dreamed of your taste. Woke up so hard, I'd stroke my dick just to get some kind of relief."

She gasped.

Graham removed the thin material from her thighs. He moaned before settling himself between her legs. "Finally, after all this time."

His warm breath floated over her clit. The small nub pulsed and her pussy clenched. What the hell was he waiting for? She wanted to force him to get to work, but he seemed content to stare at her.

"Graham," she whined. "You're killing me."

He chuckled then placed a kiss on her folds. His tongue drew the small pearl into his mouth. Each suck of his mouth shot straight through her. Desire built low in her belly, growing more intense with each pull. Elle wrapped her legs around his waist while she held his face to her. He'd barely begun, and she already sat on edge. His tongue slid through her folds and pushed into her.

She bucked.

As he continued to take his fill of her, his arm held her in place, adding to the sensations washing over her. She couldn't believe how quickly things escalated, but she wouldn't do it any differently. Holding onto him, he took her higher. He nibbled and sucked on her sensitive flesh, turning her into a puddle of goo. His moans vibrated against her skin, and her eyes rolled up into her head.

With his arm across her stomach, he reached up, palming her breast. His fingers pinched and tugged on her hard nipple, adding to the blissful pleasure. She rolled her hips, trying to direct his ministrations, but he'd have none of it. He growled. His slate-blue gaze locked with hers, as he feasted on her. He sipped from her with such vigor it jolted her senses. When he added first one finger then a second, she lost it. Elle cried out as her climax shot through her. The swiftness of it startled her.

"Mmm, fuck yes. Give it to me." He continued to finger her through her release, drawing out the ripples of her climax. Limp and sated, she let out a soft sigh. Graham gave a rumbled chuckle while placing a final kiss to her sex. "We're nowhere near done, beautiful." The wicked gleam in his eyes turned her on as he climbed up her body. "Ready?"

She nodded, unable to vocalize her needs. His tongue thrust into her mouth at the same moment he filled her. Shocking pain flared inside of her, as she tried to adjust to his girth. He stilled, his breath coming in short pants. A pained expression filled his feature. "Graham?"

"Fuck," he grunted. "You're so damn snug. Give me a second."

She laughed softly. "Give you a second? You're impaling me with a rod."

He hissed. "Don't laugh." His hand fit between them, and he

swiped her clit with his thumb. Her hips shifted. "That's it, beautiful. Relax."

She clamped down on him; the muscles of her pussy rippled around him. When he retreated slightly, she tried to hold him inside her. "Oh my."

Their pace started out slow. She relished the exquisite drag of his cock through her sensitive folds. The juxtaposition between the graceful way he ignited her body and the power contained within his muscular form, blew her away. She caressed the muscles of his shoulders while kissing his neck, silently encouraging him.

The sound of his grunts destroyed any semblance of control she might have held onto. She fell into the rhythm of their lovemaking, giving over to the raw emotions flowing between them. "Hey now." He swiped away her tears. She stared up at him. The unfettered love in his gaze obliterated her. "I should have told you then, but I mean to tell you every day for the rest of my life how much I love you." He pressed his lips to hers.

He moved with urgency then. The rock of their bodies growing more desperate. Fire built inside her, pushing them headlong into release. She clung to him. Her nails dug into his flesh, and she knew the way he gripped her hips, she'd wear his mark as well. She sank into the feeling of him powering in and out of her. Their sighs and moans mingled, adding to the already-erotic atmosphere surrounding them. Lost in their own sanctuary, she let go. She soared in his arms. Her muscles rippled around him as a keen whine passed her lips. The rush of her orgasm shattered her.

Graham stilled within her. When the waves of her release subsided, he began again, this time with single-minded focus. He fucked her ruthlessly. His hips slammed against hers while his fingers found her clit once more. He worked that hard bud, his tongue flicking against her neck. The harsh masculine sounds he made ramped her back up. Wound tighter than a spring she cried out, meeting him thrust for thrust.

A harsh snarl vibrated in his chest seconds before his teeth locked on her neck. She screamed as he filled her twice more then stilled. The heat of his release bathed her in warmth while she continued to spasm around him. "Mine."

He pulled her to him, rolling them so she was sprawled across him. "I love you, too."

***

Graham walked into Shawn's office the next morning, confused as to why he'd been called there. A sleeping Elle lay in his bed after they continued their mating at his home, the ring she'd worn since arriving home, discarded. They'd have to deal with it at some point, but, for the moment, he was content to spend time with his mate and build the trust and love they had for one another.

Taking a seat, he waited while the PI finished his phone call. On the desk sat a manila envelope with Elle's name on it. Curious to its contents, he reached for it. However, his hand was stilled by Shawn's.

"We should talk about this first." Shawn removed his hand from Graham's.

"Okay."

"Miss Kathy came to me a few days ago and asked for some help," he started. "She thought it was pretty unusual this Rupert guy hadn't called Elle, or tried to find her like Kizzy has. So, she asked me to do a little snooping."

His gut knotted. In a way, he needed to know what lay inside that package, and, in another way, no matter if he and Elle were mates, the news might devastate her. "What did you find?"

"Tons. I can say it's a good thing she got away when she did." Opening the envelope, he pulled out several eight-by-ten photographs then what amounted to a court indictment.

Graham looked at every picture. Rupert, it seemed, had a hidden girlfriend. The brunette at his side for several galas was covered in expensive jewelry and expensive dresses. Though, in the following pictures, money meant nothing to the man, as Rupert tore the gown from the woman and proceeded to fuck her against the window of their hotel room. Anger flowed through his veins. Elle had given this piece of shit the greatest gift, and he'd gone and thrown it away for some sleazy woman.

"The paperwork is worse." Shawn's voice cut through the rage building within him.

"I bet," he snarled. Picking up the document, he read through it. Some of it might not have made sense to him, since it was legalese, but money laundering, insider trading, and corruption made perfect sense to him. In total, there were thirty-four counts which were under the RICO, Racketeer Influenced and Corrupt Organizations

Act, as well. Shocked, he sat there for a moment. Would Elle be caught up in any of this? Not that it mattered—no one would ever find her—but he knew her sense of duty and her loyalty would demand she be held accountable if she'd been privy to any of his dealings. "Shit."

"My guy says Rupert was picked up a month before I contacted Elle. I don't think she has a clue. In fact, I don't think anyone knows about Elle. Or the house he owns in Charlotte, where she stays. This guy has connections. Deep, sinister connections. I am betting, if I dig deeper, there are more women involved, and potentially a wife."

He shook his head. How did Elle not know? "Don't. This is enough."

"I wasn't going to, unless she asked me to," Shawn admitted. "I don't know how she didn't know about this, but I believe he left her in a secluded part of Charlotte, oblivious to his activities. A late business trip here. An all-night meeting there. Or send her and Kizzy on a small vacation. You can cover up everything. There are ways to make all this go away."

"I'll have to tell her. She needs to know the truth."

Shawn shrugged. "I don't know. If you've mated her, which"— he pointed to Graham's neck—"looks like you did, she might not care."

No. Not my Elle. She might have taken off that ring, but she didn't forget, and he figured deep down she held some guilt and self-recrimination. "I have to tell her the truth."

"Have it your way, but I believe you'll hurt her more than help her." He placed the stuff back into the envelope.

"Yeah, maybe. But, I think, in this situation, knowing the truth will help ease her guilt, even if she won't vocalize her feelings to me. She's fought them since she got off the bus. Last night, she gave in to the possibility. Today, she'll realize her wolf and heart always knew the truth." He took the proffered packet from Shawn then stood. "Thanks for the help, even though I wasn't looking for it."

"Eh, thank Miss Kathy." He shrugged.

Graham nodded. "I'll send her a card or something," he replied sarcastically.

Shawn laughed. "Don't be too hard on her. Her heart is in the right place, and so is her gut, which turned out to be correct."

"Yeah, I know. It's what makes this a tougher pill to swallow."

"True."

With a lift of his hand, he exited the office and headed back to his truck. The irritating itch of knowing he had to tell Elle clawed at the back of his neck. Nevertheless, he had no clue how to even broach the subject, or if, like Shawn supposed, he should keep it to himself, and never tell her. Though not a lie, if she ever found the photographs, or if by chance Miss Kathy ever told her, she'd know he kept it from her, and it'd hurt her more in the long run. The catch-22 he'd been put into stung like a bitch. So, he needed a plan. He needed a way to strengthen their foundation, to lessen the blow of this major breach of trust on Rupert's part. He had to show her, no matter what, she'd always been worthy of love—his love. Not some criminal asshole's.

Getting into his truck, he tucked the paperwork into the middle seat console then started the engine. He pulled away from the curb and headed back to the ranch. Today, they'd go for a run.

Chapter Nine

The time she spent with Lily, Fawn, and Gabby had done Elle some good. However, she waited for the guilt to overwhelm her. To drown her in contrition. Though she felt horrible about not telling Kizzy the truth, Ryker was right—the safety of the pack came first. She wanted to talk to Graham about that. Maybe they could find someone for Kizzy. Happiness filled her. She knew a couple of wolves right up her alley who could make her as happy as she was.

The sense of rightness beat back any negative feeling she might have had over sleeping with Graham, even though she'd taken off her engagement ring and they were, for all intents and purposes, mates.

The mark at the juncture of her shoulder and neck tingled. *Mate.* A peacefulness washed over her.

"There it is," Fawn teased. "That smile."

Heat suffused her cheeks. "What can I say?"

The door opened a few minutes later, and Graham stepped over the threshold. Tension rode his shoulders, before that easy smile of his slid into place. He pulled his hat off and hung it up then strolled over to where she sat.

He held his hand out to her. "How would you like to go for a run?"

"Right now?"

"We'll stay on the property. We have plenty of trails here, and some even lead back into town." He helped her up then guided her through the kitchen and out the back door. Once they were away from the house, they started the hike out to his favorite trail.

"Finally, we're alone."

He shucked his clothes first then called to the wolf within him, allowing the shift to come over him. His bones displaced then realigned. When his perspective changed, he sat and waited while Elle shifted.

He padded to her and rubbed his side against hers. With a yip, he took off, following the trail toward the creek. It had been the one place they could be alone before everything in their lives got turned upside down.

They climbed the ridge, zigging and zagging between the trees, never pushing too hard. So many good memories had taken place there. They stopped beside one of the giant spruce trees. Moss clung to the rocks at the banks, while pine needles and sprigs of grass poked through the wet fertile ground. The sunlight shimmered on the crystal-clear water, giving the area a majestic glow. While they stood their together, he knew with a deep-seated conviction he had to tell Elle the truth. He'd love to keep the bullshit Shawn's guy found away from her for the rest of her life, but she needed to make a clean break. She deserved to know, she hadn't done anything wrong, and each moment of her life in Charlotte had prepared her for this.

After lazing by the stream watching the minnows catching flies and the bees dance from flower to flower, pollenating them as they went, Shawn led them on their way home. The sun touched the horizon when they finally stepped up onto the porch once more.

When he pulled open the door, the cheerful greeting from his family assailed them. At some point, Gabby had showed up with Kru in tow, and Lily had started dinner for them. He knew they might be overwhelming Elle, but she needed to get used to it. They were all about family. His parents wouldn't demand any less. In fact, they'd be pretty damn proud. They'd also be overjoyed to see she lived.

Chapter Ten

E lle woke to the sensual kisses Graham placed along her shoulder blade. The decadence had her skin tingling and her body heating to his touch. Last night had been a ball. After dinner, they grabbed her things from Kathy's place then went into town for a little get-together Drew had insisted the pack needed in order to connect with one another. He'd been right.

They laughed and danced and talked about the old ways, and the new ways. They remembered those they'd lost—which had her thinking about her friend and the lie hanging between them. Though she knew the whys and hows, she hated not telling Kizzy the truth. She trusted her friend. No matter what. Yet, without a mate, her friend couldn't join her. Determination filled her. She'd fix this. Like she'd fixed everything with Graham.

Rolling over, she greeted her mate with a smile. His heavy-lidded gaze seared every inch of her as he peered down at her. Her wolf languished in his attention, finally feeling whole again, and not the broken soul she'd become. Elle hadn't realized in the years she'd been gone, she'd actually hurt herself. She'd hobbled her wolf to the point, the first time she shifted, it felt like all of her bones snapped in two. The sheer agony of it had her crying out for relief as everything inside her realigned. By the time she returned to Miss Kathy's house, she'd dreaded the shift back to her human form but knew the momentary pain would ease and she'd never ignore or abuse her wolf again.

"Good morning." She reached up to cup his cheek. "Did you sleep well?"

He gave her a lazy grin, and wrapped his free arm around her middle, tucking her to his side. "I did. Even better waking up next to you." He dipped his head and took her lips in a passionate kiss. He teased her. Tempted her. Their tongues tangled together as a soft moan fell from her lips.

Shifting their positions, he fitted his hips between hers. The gentle rock of his body fanned the embers of her arousal, setting her ablaze within seconds. The plea to take her, give in to the hedonistic pleasure, sat on the tip of her tongue as he lined himself up, and thrust deep within her in one stroke. Her back arched and a surprised whimper fell from her lips. He stretched her so perfectly, reaching every inch of her, mind, body, and soul.

The easy glide of their body hadn't been too fast or too slow. It consumed her. Freed her. The grip he had on her hips tightened as he whispered her name with a groan. Face buried in her neck, the soft grunts of pleasure he made were like pinpricks of desire dancing along her nerve endings, ramping up the need flowing through her. She wrapped her arms around his neck, and trailed her fingers up and down the tensed muscles of his shoulders. Yes, she was exactly where she was meant to be.

"So fucking perfect," he murmured against the shell of her ear. "I'll never get enough of you."

"Nor I, you." She placed a kiss to his shoulder.

Their lazy pace continued, until they grew frantic. The knot of bliss wound tighter in her belly, threatening to consume her whole. The planes of Graham's face grew fiercer, while the apples of his cheeks turned a deeper shade of pink, enhancing his freckles. The wolf stared down at her. His slate-blue eyes stunned her with their captivating hue. The veins at his neck were corded with the strain at which he held himself back.

Elle fingered his nipple, and a shudder worked through him. She knew he battled himself, making sure to take care of her first. She kissed and licked the mark she left on his neck the first night of their mating. His thrusts became unhinged. His pace erratic. He lowered his face again and nuzzled her neck, mouthing the sensitive area. Electricity sizzled and spread outward, like fingers of need. He did it again then growled. The minute he bit down, she did as well. Her release shot through her, stealing her senses and leaving her reeling. Above her, he shivered and continued to rock into her body, extending their pleasure.

When he finally gathered her in his arms, he placed a kiss to her temple. The way he held her had her sighing. Always strong and always protective of her. "We need to talk." He kissed her again. She tensed in his embrace. "I promise we will be okay."

She pushed up to stare down at him. "What's going on?"

"Stay here." He slid out of bed, giving her a glorious glimpse of his ass before he covered it with his jeans. He opened the door to their room and disappeared. A few minutes later, he returned, a package in his hand. He closed the door behind him then crossed the room to her side. "What you see in here is in no way a reflection of you."

"I'll be the judge of that." She took the manila envelope. Her stomach soured.

"If I had it my way, you'd never see it."

All the peaceful, intimate feelings of a few minutes ago were gone. Her heart hammered. Her brain raced, trying to figure out what the hell was going on. She opened the envelope and dumped the contents on the bed in front of her.

There, glossy black-and-white photographs showed Rupert and another woman standing outside some event. Another of them in a hotel room. Picture after picture, she saw what her heart had denied so many times. Had told her. She was foolish to believe a man like Rupert would never cheat on her. *Well, he is, after all, only human.* She knew the women in the photos. She'd worked with her before on some charity her ex-fiancé put together to keep her busy. She'd hated the woman instantly. Now, she knew why.

I've been a fool. Why was she the one who'd worn his ring? Why did he have to choose her out of all the little hussies he obviously kept on the side? *Is it because I'm safe? Unsuspecting? Stupid? Gullible?* As she pushed the photos out of the way, she found a thick document below. "What's this?"

"An indictment. Did Rupert disappear for a time?" He didn't touch her. Gave her room to process what she read, and see for herself. To form her own opinion of the situation. She loved him even more for it, but she couldn't help the rage burning her gut. Her stomach churned.

She thought back to the date listed on the documents. She and Kizzy had gone on a retreat. There had been some press surrounding Rupert, but she'd never given it a second thought—heck, she never paid attention to the press following him. When she returned home, he'd been there waiting for her. He'd asked about her weekend away, taken her to dinner, and never once gave a hint of what had happened or that he was in trouble. He'd also been a good liar. She'd never known. Or, she'd been so oblivious to it all, she hadn't cared. God, she was a fool.

"Probably. Kizzy and I went on a girls' weekend on this date. I guess he could have been picked up while I wasn't there." Numbed by the infractions listed on the document, she felt like an idiot. How had she not known this? How had she been so ignorant to the news? She shook her head. *Laundering. Bribes. Insider trading. Cheater. A regular good guy.* She threw the indictment on the bed in disgust. "How did you find this?"

"Shawn gave it to me."

"So, what? You went snooping when you knew I was engaged?" All rationality flew out the door. Even though she knew he didn't have anything to do with Rupert being an asshole, he got the brunt of it. "Y-you thought you knew what's best for me?"

"Whoa." He held up his hands. "I had no part of this. It was the matrons. They wanted you to know the truth. Shawn helped them, and I got this dropped in my lap. But I won't say I blame them. He's an asshole. He would have taken you down his depraved rabbit hole given half the chance."

"How do you know I'm not already down the hole?" How many of those charges could be pinned on her? How many on his family? Were they all corrupt? Questions swirled around questions. "Why in God's name would the matrons do this? I was here. I came home."

"You also wanted to leave," he countered. "You were ready to give it all up and be a human for the rest of your life or whatever the hell you were going to do."

"So they were going to push my life in the direction they wanted it to go?" She couldn't believe them. So she'd been a little confused and thought she knew what she wanted when she'd arrived. She'd been gone for over ten years. What the hell was wrong with people?

"I think they wanted to give you the other side of the coin and let you know what was going on. I don't think they meant any harm."

She gathered everything and placed it back into the envelope. "Well, we'll see about that."

Throwing the sheet back, she got out of bed and stormed to her bag. After grabbing her clothes, she stomped into the bathroom, uncaring if she didn't have a stitch of clothes on. No way in hell she'd let those nosy women interfere with her life. She turned on the water and waited for it to warm. Though she hadn't heard about this stuff till after she'd mated Graham, she didn't like people meddling in her life. No matter what, a part of her had known she'd end up with him. Well, her wolf always knew, even if it took her mind a little bit to wrap about the fact he, too, lived and desired her.

Stepping under the spray, she tried to calm the anger welling up in her. She tried to be rational about what they did. She owed Ryker her life. However, it didn't mean Miss Kathy could stick her nose into affairs she had no business messing with.

She soaped up her hair then rinsed and finished her shower. When she got out, a cup of coffee waited for her on the sink. *Graham.* God, she'd been such a shit to him, after he'd made love to her, and he'd been honest and showed her. She'd have understood if he'd burned the information instead.

Once she'd dressed and pulled her hair back, she headed downstairs to the kitchen. The place had cleared out. Even Fawn hadn't been sitting on the couch. *Shit. You've hurt everyone's feelings.* Well, maybe not their feelings so much as their hospitality. She felt like a piece of dried bull dung. Placing the half-empty mug in the sink, she headed out. She knew where the women were most of the time, but this early, she wasn't sure. Knowing the walk to town wouldn't take long, it gave her a chance to gather her thoughts. Just holding the evidence in her hand, made her sick to her stomach. Her gut knotted.

Yes, a walk would do her good. As she stepped out of the house, Graham sat by the fence line on his paint mare. He looked sad. A bit mule kicked. *Shit.* She'd taken this crap out on him, and it wasn't his fault. Hurrying to his side, she stopped in front of him. Running her hand along the mare's nose, she gazed up at him. "I'm sorry. I shouldn't have gotten mad at you. All of this is such an...upheaval, you know?"

He nodded and dismounted his horse. "I know, honey. I know." He wrapped her in his arms and his scent blanketed her, chasing away her wayward thoughts.

Breathing deep, she nuzzled his neck. "Forgive me?"

"Of course. There was never anything to forgive." He tipped her chin up and kissed her. "I love you. You're my mate."

"I love you. You're my mate, too." She kissed him again then untangled from him. "I'll be in town. See you in a few hours." She left Graham by the entrance to the pastureland and headed for town.

When she was far enough away from her mate, her thoughts returned to Rupert. Maybe she should have known he was the kind of man described in the pages. Should have known about the case pending against him. But she never went to any of those fancy parties with him. She never stayed in that hotel where he screwed the girl by the window. She never had tons of jewelry draped over her body. Nothing. Yet she'd worn the ring. She'd agreed to marry him. And the entire time Rupert pursued her, she'd fought the truth—her heart and wolf belonged to one man. Her only excuse was believing she would never set foot in Los Lobos again.

Yet, if she hadn't gone to Charlotte, she wouldn't have met Kizzy. She wouldn't have lived a better life than what she would've here. She'd have been broken and battered. She'd have lived a life filled with fear and despair. No, each step she'd taken after the night she got on the bus was meant to bring her back to her pack. Back to her home.

So, should she be mad at the matrons? No. Miss Kathy believed she was doing the right thing. Elle appreciated it. But the mistakes of her life were hers. Thankfully, Elle had known nothing of Rupert's business dealings. Whatever he got into, he did it on his own.

As she came around the bend, Los Lobos laid out before her, a sense of calm washed over her. Though she understood the whys and hows, she still didn't need the matrons sticking their noses where they didn't belong. She was a big girl. She could take care of herself.

She eased down the wooden walkway toward the only open door to Ginger and Kole's store. She stepped inside. The ladies perused a rack of books. Elle glanced around until she found Miss Kathy to the right, reading the back cover of a book.

"Well, you're not hard to find." She approached them.

"We're not hiding, dear," Miss Fern replied.

"You couldn't leave well enough alone, could you?" She held out the packet to Miss Kathy. "Had to dig around."

She sniffed. "I was right, wasn't I?"

"It doesn't matter if you're right." Elle sighed. "You stuck your nose in somewhere it didn't belong."

"You would have hemmed and hawed over this for who knows how long, child." She eased around the other side of the shelf. "You'd have continued to lie to yourself and to your wolf. You would have continued to deny your mate."

"No," Elle retorted.

"No?"

"Whatever." She swallowed the lump of guilt at her assertion.

"Don't sass," Miss Claire admonished. "It's unbecoming."

"We only meant to help you," Miss Fern added. "We're not trying to be mean."

She growled. "I know. I'm grateful for the information. I didn't need it, though."

"No?" Miss Kathy arched a brow. "Why's that?"

"You know why." Her cheeks heated. "I needed a minute is all."

"You needed a swift kick in your ass," Miss Lonnie quipped. "I'm sure we could do it again if you'd like."

She laughed. "No, I'm good."

When a wolf the size of a house walked through the door, Miss Kathy's face lit up. Sayer Blackcrow nodded to the matron. *I'll be damned.* He was built like a wolf who could tear a smaller man limb from limb, had a swagger about him, but a kindness, too. He wore jeans and a black skin-tight shirt. She could count each and every abdominal muscle. Tattoos crisscrossed his forearms and climbed up his biceps. Oh yes, this specimen rivaled Kru, big time.

"Oh there you are." Miss Kathy sauntered to him and took his hand. "I am so glad you could meet us here."

"Not a problem, ma'am." The deep, angry growl of his voice held an edge of warning. And if his posture was any indication, he really didn't want to be there. However, no one told the matrons no. "I'll have that elk to Henry later this afternoon."

"Such a good boy." Miss Fern grinned. "He'll be a pleased wolf."

"Anything I can do to help." He turned from the group to exit the store.

"One more thing." Miss Kathy grinned. "I talked with Graham this morning when he was at the convenience store. Seems Elle has been going to town and he can't go with her all the time."

Elle stilled.

"Ma'am?"

"Well, you are a protector," she stated. "If you were to follow her on occasion, not get in the way, you know, I think it would make her mate breathe a little easier. You know how some humans can be."

His lip curled, and his eyes darkened with a deadly intent. "I understand. No one will see me and I will not interfere. Good day."

He stalked out of the shop, leaving Elle to gape at him.

"Well now, he's one hunk of a wolf." Miss Lonnie came up beside her friend.

"What the hell just happened?" Elle glanced between the women.

Miss Claire patted her hand. "Relax, dear. No sense in worrying. Everything will work out fine."

"Just fine," Miss Fern added.

As much as she'd hoped to set up Kizzy, she hadn't wanted to do it this way. The wolf would hate her friend. "Somehow, I think you've made a mess of everything."

Epilogue

Two months later....

Elle sat at her desk in Brie's office and checked the schedule. For the next hour, her boss had free time. In the last couple of months, a few more wolves had come home, and there were several new mates. Plus, she got to see Kizzy whenever she wanted.

When her friend realized she wouldn't be returning to Charlotte, she'd put her house on the market and moved into a small apartment in Custer. Unbeknownst to Elle, Kizzy had a trust fund from her late parents'. She worked with special needs kids because she wanted to, not for the money.

God, the things she'd learned about her friend in the last two months.... She felt like she didn't really know Kizzy. But then, the same could be said about her, she supposed. Elle still worried, if her friend ever found out the truth, she'd lose her. She didn't want that.

After going to Rapid City for a day trip, Sayer following them but staying out of sight, they saw on the news what Rupert had really been up to. His company had been laundering money used in a sex trade business. The insider trading had been for cancer drugs—drugs he'd helped drive up the cost on. Drugs meant for children fighting neuroblastoma. The more information they found out, the more it made both of them sick. Sitting inside the café, drinking their lattes, they made a pact to never utter his name again. And, they agreed, the foul bastard needed to rot in jail for the rest of his life.

After shutting down her laptop, she grabbed her jacket and

headed for the door. Graham wanted to meet her at the diner for lunch. The man barely let her out of his sight, and who could blame him? They'd been apart for over ten years, and she didn't want to leave his side either.

Taking her seat on the bus going to Charlotte all those years ago—afraid of everything and worried about what would happen next—she'd only known the way of the pack. Not about the snakes who never changed form in the human world. Like Rupert.

But that was her past. Today, she could see her future, with her pack and her very best friend.

Stepping outside, she took a deep breath and grinned. Summer in the hills could be overly warm or tepid. A cool breeze blew in from the north, blending comfortably with the heat of the midday sun.

Lifting her face, she allowed the warmth to seep into her pores. Around her, the forest sang, alive with activity. Birds chirped while scavengers scurried across the thicket floor. She stepped off the porch and began the short trek to town. She enjoyed working with Brie, helping wolves, being part of something greater. It felt pretty good.

She walked down the dirt trail that quickly became a paved path, past the small park being built near the center of town. She'd heard through the grapevine that the Burrows child, Jessie, had requested someplace to play. Drew had granted the request, and construction had begun. Seemed so strange to see all the changes. After witnessing firsthand the destruction of her pack, to see the life and soul of it return...excited her.

As she neared Dottie's, the door to the diner stood open, waiting for the next customer. Elle crossed the street and entered the building. The place appeared empty. *Weird.* She glanced at the clock on the wall and noted the time. There should have been a rush of pack mates grabbing lunch before going back to work. Instead, the place mimicked an abandoned building.

"Hello?" she called out, concerned at not seeing Birdie. The elderly woman always greeted every customer. She'd heard about the woman's health scare and the fragility of cancer, even in remission. She worried. "Anyone here?"

"Elle?" Graham's deep voice vibrated through her, and she turned to face him.

He held a single red rose in his hand. Behind him, members of their pack gathered.

"Graham, what's going on?"

"Twelve years ago, a bright-eyed girl enchanted a scrawny wannabe cowboy. She was all pigtails and pretty dresses." He pulled out a photo of them and showed it to everyone around them.

She remembered the day vividly. Her mother had just bought the camera and waited to try it out. She took pictures of everything.

"The minute she tucked herself into my side, I knew she was the wolf for me." He strode to her, allowing the others to enter the diner with him. "You told me that day, it was the best day ever." He pushed a lock of her hair behind her ear. "You were right."

Elle gasped when he placed the photo into her hand.

"You kept it," she whispered. "After everything."

"Well of course I kept it. When we left town, I stared at this picture and told myself what happened just a few short days before couldn't be true. My heart and mind warred day and night. I knew you were alive—the bond connecting us snapped together the minute you put your arms around me. But my mind told me you were gone. I saw your house. I smelled the fire, and the awful stench of death clinging to everything, including our clothes. I thought I'd die. I prepared for it. I wrote letters to everyone. My mom and dad. Kalum and Lily. I told them how much I loved them and how much more I loved you. I accepted the coming day when my heart would cease to beat and I'd finally be with you again. That day never came. I lived. For ten years I worked and strived. I tried to reconcile what was going on. Again, my heart insisted you lived, while my mind told me no. To let it go and move on. I couldn't."

Elle stared at him, surprise mixed with curiosity along with a little anxiousness. "What...what is this all about?" She licked her lips, glancing up at him.

"I'm getting there." He smiled at her. "Then, a couple of months ago, Shawn asked me to do a favor for him. Go to Hill City and pick up a returning wolf. I didn't understand why he asked me to do it, but I went. A pack mate coming home is a big deal around here after everything. The bus pulled up to the sign, and the doors opened. For long moments, I stood there waiting. I thought maybe he'd been mistaken."

Soft chuckles filled the space as more and more people filled the diner. She didn't know what the heck was going on, but she felt the love of her pack surrounding her. It overwhelmed her while also solidifying her place.

"I saw Elle. My heart stopped. The two parts of me, the head and heart, after all this time, stopped bickering, and the wolf within me pushed forward. My mate had returned. My mate had survived."

He pulled the ring out of his pocket, held it up for all to see. Excitement threatened to overwhelm her.

"When we lived with the humans, I learned a thing or two." He smirked as he got down on one knee. "Women love romance. They love knowing they belong and are wanted. I want you to understand, and believe, I love you and you belong with me. We're mates and nothing will ever break our bond. On those long lonely nights, it was you I thought about. So, now I ask you to do me one more favor."

"Anything."

"Marry me."

The enthusiastic, audible gasp surrounding them made her laugh.

"Well?"

"What in the world are you doing?" Thrown off-balance she knelt with him, unable to assimilate what she was experiencing. The love she had for Graham transcended everything. She knew, deep down, he was the only one. She knew she'd settled, thinking she'd never come home. Never have her mate. In fact, she'd given up on herself and her pack. She never told anyone, yet the feeling had been there. Now, she couldn't imagine her life outside of this place.

"Isn't it obvious?"

"You're nuts," she whispered, taking his hands into hers. "Marry you?"

"Yep. I like being a modern guy."

She laughed, taking the ring out of his hand. "Modern, huh?" She gazed at the ring, taking in the details. It was beautiful. Nothing like the overcompensating rock he-who-shall-never-be-talked-about-ever-again gave her. The one carat princess-cut diamond sat on a simple titanium band. "I suppose I could marry you."

He growled. "You suppose?"

She shrugged. "Yeah, I guess so." She placed the ring on her finger and looked at it.

"You guess so? Woman!" He tugged her to him then pressed his lips to hers. He commanded her with the kiss, showing her how much he desired her and what happened when she teased his wolf.

"Yes," she murmured, a little breathless. "I'd have agreed the minute you started, but you kept going on and on and on."

Graham stood then threw her over his shoulder. "If you'll excuse us." He smacked her ass. "I have to show my little mate here a thing or two."

Elle laughed. "Such a brute." He smacked her ass again. "Ouch."

"Don't worry, mate. I promise to kiss it better," he grunted, walking toward the door.

"I said yes, by the way."

He allowed her to slide down his body until she stood in front of him. "I know you did. I love you, Elle St. Claire."

"I love you, too, Graham Truesdale."

"I'm still going to spank your ass."

"I wouldn't have it any other way." Elle smiled. "But, first, you'll have to catch me."

She darted for the door and ran for the woods. The howl of triumph from her mate spurred her on.

She howled in answer then laughed as she kicked it into overdrive. Her home was in the hills of South Dakota. She'd remain in Los Lobos for the rest of her life with Graham by her side and any children they were gifted with. Life, for her, was pretty damn perfect.

Yes, this is where I belong.

About the Author

TL Reeve, a multi-published author with Cobblestone Press, Decadent Publishing, Evernight Publishing, and Loose-Id, was born out of a love of family and a bond that became unbreakable. Living in Alabama, TL misses Los Angeles, and will one day return to the beaches of Southern California to ride the waves at Huntington Beach. When not writing something hot and sexy, TL can be found curled up with a good book, or working on homework with a cute little pixie.

You can signup for her newsletter at: http://eepurl.com/bvo7fn

Also by TL Reeve